# The Secret Billionaire's Missing Date

## By

## Dee Markwith

## Contents

# Chapter One
## *Vanessa*

*Well, this is a total disaster,* Vanessa thought as she sat across the table from her date. As with her previous dates, she'd agreed to meet at the busy coffee shop in downtown Manhattan that she knew and trusted. She felt safe here, knowing she wouldn't be alone with a man she'd never met before, and reassured by the shop's security cameras. In broad daylight, surrounded by other patrons, this was the place she preferred to meet her dates for the first time.

This was the fifth man she'd met online, and if she thought the others were duds, this guy definitely took the cake. She was trying not to stare as she mentally compared Harold to his profile pictures on *Plenty of Fish*, the dating site she'd been trying with little success. The man sitting opposite her looked ten years older and fifty pounds heavier than his online photos, and she could smell his body odor over the aroma of her coffee. He'd tried to hide his thinning hair with a bad comb-over, and the thick lenses of his glasses were housed by frames that had gone out of style decades earlier. He was a messy wreck of a man who acted as awkward as he looked.

His well-written profile had impressed her enough to warrant a reply, but she was quickly realizing just how much he'd changed himself. He'd described himself as an elementary school teacher living in a modest apartment on the Lower East Side, yet his story unraveled as he clumsily opened up about his life.

"I'm, well, I'm technically not a school teacher yet," he told her as he nervously fidgeted with his glasses. "I work for the school district, though."

"Oh? Doing what?" she asked politely, having no genuine interest in the answer. She knew the moment he'd joined her at her table that this was the last time she'd ever see him. So far, nobody had been worthy of a second date, and he was no exception. She didn't think it was asking too much for somebody to be open and honest with her. All four of her previous dates had greatly exaggerated their lives, and this guy had heavily embellished his as well.

"I'm a bus driver right now," he confessed, adding, "but I want to be a teacher someday. I'm thinking about going to school for it soon. I just need to get back on my feet."

"Right, get back on your feet," she repeated, trying to feign interest.

"I had back surgery last year and couldn't work. I had to move back in with my mom. I'll be getting my own place again soon if all goes well. I just need to save up."

"Well, I hope that works out for you," she replied, hoping she didn't sound as dishonest as she thought she did. Scooping up her purse, she asked, "Can you excuse me for a second? I need to use the ladies' room."

He nodded politely, his hands wrapped around his cup of coffee as he watched her make her way to the restroom. Locking the door behind her, she groaned loudly and dropped her purse on the counter. She looked at herself in the mirror, silently chastising herself for being so stupid. If the previous four dates didn't work out, why did she think this one would be any different?

The guy had seemed nice enough and had come across as grounded and stable. Though he wasn't a looker by any means, his pictures hadn't been terrible. She'd never considered herself a shallow woman and could overlook physical shortcomings if a man treated her well. She loved kids so much that she dreamed of opening her own daycare one day and had been drawn in by this guy's talk of being an elementary school teacher. Though he did work with kids, it wasn't precisely in the capacity he'd claimed, and he'd obviously been disingenuous with his pictures.

While she wasn't a superficial person, she did have standards, and personal hygiene was one of them. He looked and smelled like he hadn't bathed in a week and his button-up shirt was wrinkled and stained. *A first impression is a lasting one*, her mother had always told her. If this was his idea of a good first impression, he clearly had a few screws loose.

Like her other four dates, she'd made every attempt to look presentable and thought she'd done a damn good job. Looking at her reflection again, she noted how her yellow summer dress contrasted nicely against her dark skin. The dress highlighted her curves, and the slit on the right side allowed her to show off a bit of leg without being too revealing. She'd accentuated her big, brown eyes with gold eyeshadow, and her eyeliner was on point. She'd taken the time to curl her long, black hair and added a cute yellow flower clip. Her heels even matched the outfit, and her purse did as well. She'd turned some heads in the coffee shop, assuring her that she looked as good as she felt. Meanwhile, her date had shown up looking like he'd picked his clothes up off of the floor.

"Way to waste your time, girl," she sighed to herself as she dug through her purse and found her cell phone. It was time for Doug to save her for the fifth and, hopefully, final time. She'd tried the online dating thing, and it had been a monumental failure. With that in mind, she resolved to delete her profile when she got home since every date had been miserable. The first guy didn't give her a chance to speak, going on and on about himself as she sat in disbelief at his motor mouth. The second tried too hard, and she cringed at every awful attempt he made to make her laugh. The third had been using pictures that weren't even of him and dared to ask her to pay for his coffee. The fourth confessed that he'd served a few years in prison for armed robbery when he was younger. At least they'd bathed and attempted to dress nice.

She wished she had the free time needed to meet men in the real world like she used to before she'd been promoted and her job had consumed her life. Working as a manager for a call center was more demanding than it sounded, and with a mortgage to pay, she needed all the hours she could get.

"Hey, girl, hey!" Doug answered in his usual singsong fashion.

"You know the drill," Vanessa told him, unable to guise the disappointment in her voice.

"That bad, huh?"

"Uh, yeah. If you could bail me out again, I'll love you forever. This will be the last time, I swear."

"You know I got you," Doug replied. "Five minutes?"

"Five minutes."

"I want all the details later."

"I'll call you the second I'm out of here," she assured him.

Ending the call, she slipped her phone back into her purse. She'd met Doug Henson at work three years earlier, and he'd quickly become her best friend. He was a short, overweight man with an effeminate voice, and although he'd never admit it, she was fairly sure he was gay. He'd never shown any interest in women; as far as she knew, he hadn't gone on any dates. He was a bit of an oddball, but they'd hit it off and bonded over similar interests. In fact, she was surprised by how much they had in common. When she told him she crocheted in her little spare time, he shared that he crocheted as well. When she told him she had two cats, he delighted in telling her about his two feline roommates. When she told him she was shamefully addicted to the show *Days of Our Lives*, he confessed that he was also a fan. Between those three things, she didn't need to question why he had no girlfriend.

After her first *Plenty of Fish* date with the blabbermouth, she realized she'd need an escape plan for future meet-ups and recruited Doug's help. Together, they devised a method of extracting her from disaster dates. She'd inform him ahead of time that she was meeting with somebody so he'd know to have his phone on him. If things went south, she'd excuse herself to the restroom and call him. Five minutes later, he'd call her back, pretending to be her brother and claiming there was a medical emergency with their mother. This way, she wouldn't be rude by texting from the table. She also wouldn't risk her date catching a glimpse of what she was writing. She didn't want to hurt anyone's feelings if she could avoid it.

Their plan had worked perfectly the first three times, giving her no reason to believe it wouldn't work now. Smoothing out her dress, she grabbed her purse and returned to the table where her date awaited her return. As with her previous three dates, she pushed her coffee aside, refusing another sip in case he'd slipped something in it. She had enough street smarts to know you never take a sip of a drink after leaving it unattended with a man you've never met before.

"Sorry about that, Harold," she smiled politely as she slipped back into her seat.

"You're gorgeous," he blurted.

Caught off guard by his unexpected compliment, Vanessa chuckled and replied, "Thank you." She paused briefly before adding, "I put a lot of time into getting ready for this."

She was hoping he'd pick up on the subtle slight. If he did, he didn't react to it. Instead, he leaned forward and said, "My mother would really like you."

"I'm sure I'd like her, too," she returned, nervously glancing around the coffee shop. She could feel his eyes on her and swallowed hard, trying to avoid his gaze. She sensed a few patrons questioning what she was doing with a guy like him and couldn't help feeling embarrassed.

"You want to come over and meet her?"

*Oh, come on. Ring, dammit, ring! Has it been five minutes yet? I can't take much more of this. You better not fuck this up, Doug. I'm counting on you.*

She pulled herself from her thoughts and deflected his question with, "Maybe. So, Harold, why don't you tell me more about yourself? What do you do for fun?"

That proved to be a great way to buy time. He told her about his love of vinyl records in painfully boring detail, and she pretended to be engaged as she waited for her phone to sound. She shifted uncomfortably in her seat, worried that Doug had gotten caught up with work and couldn't rescue her. After all, he had a shift today and had to field calls at random. If he was trapped on the phone with an unsatisfied customer, she could be stuck with Harold for a lot longer.

After what felt like an eternity, Vanessa's phone finally rang, interrupting their mind-numbingly dull conversation. "I'm so sorry, I have to take this," she told him as she eagerly grabbed her phone.

"Oh... okay."

As she carried out her act with Doug, pretending he was her brother delivering bad news about their mother, she couldn't help but notice Harold eyeing her with skepticism. Her other dates hadn't questioned the call, but Harold didn't seem so gullible. Despite his slovenly appearance and awkward mannerisms, he seemed keen to the charade she was trying to pull.

"Okay, tell her to hang in there," Vanessa continued, keeping up the ruse. "I'll be there as fast as I can. What room number? Okay, I got it. 431. Okay. I'm on my way. I love you." Ending the call, she dropped her phone back into her purse and stood to leave. "I'm so sorry," she told Harold with as much sincerity as she could muster. "My mom fell and is in rough shape. I need to go."

"Just stop," Harold hissed at her, holding one palm up.

"Excuse me?"

"Just stop with the fucking act already. I'm not an idiot."

Vanessa froze her heart beginning to race. "I don't know—"

*"Stop!"* he shouted, bringing his fist down on the table so hard their coffee cups shook and almost toppled over. The two baristas working the counter looked over with concern, as did every patron in the small shop. Harold lowered his voice and said through gritted teeth, "If I'm not good enough for you, you should have just fucking said it. You didn't have to make up some ridiculous story."

"Harold, it's not like that at all," she told him soothingly, trying to calm him down before the situation worsened. "I think you're a really nice guy, I just—"

"You women are all the same," he sneered. "You all think you're such hot shit. I hoped you were different, but you're just another whore."

His words were an instant trigger. She wasn't raised to let any man treat her with such disrespect, and anger boiled to the surface before she could stop it. "I know you didn't just call me a whore!" she snapped, getting in his face with her fist clenched.

Unfazed, Harold remained seated and looked up at her with a demented grin. "Oh, now you're going to hit me? Real nice."

"Ma'am is there a problem here?" one of the baristas approached to ask, nervously looking back and forth between Vanessa and Harold. Every customer in the shop had their eyes fixed on the unfolding scene.

Still fuming, Vanessa backed away from the table and fought to regain her composure. She typically didn't have a violent bone in her body, but she desperately wanted to punch the smirk off of Harold's face. "No, no problem," she replied, still breathing heavily. "I was just leaving."

"Ma'am, would you like us to call the cops?" the barista asked her quietly, noticing how shaken she was. She appreciated him taking her side in the situation. He'd obviously gathered that something was a bit off with the man looking up at them with a weird smile. It almost seemed as if he was enjoying himself. He casually sipped his coffee while waiting for her to answer the barista.

"Thank you, but no. I'm just going to leave," she replied.

Taking a deep breath, she collected herself and made her way to her car, muttering obscenities along the way. She hadn't been this worked up in years and was disappointed with herself for letting the man get under her skin. After giving herself another minute to calm down, she started her car and headed for home. She was still upset and knew she should have given herself another minute to cool off, but she didn't want to risk seeing him again if he left the shop. Shoving her hand into her purse, she fumbled around for her cell phone and called Doug. Thankfully, he answered on the first ring.

"Hey, girl, hey."

"Jesus, what took you so long earlier?" she asked, agitated.

"Yeah, sorry about that. Had a call, and the woman wouldn't let me off the phone. I called as soon as I could, I promise. How did it go?"

"The guy called our bluff and went nuts. Called me a whore and I almost punched him in his stupid face."

"What? No way, you're joking."

"Dead serious. Caused a scene and I thought the cops were going to get called."

"Nessa, you've got to get off that dumb dating site. It's all creepers and weirdos on there. You'd think you'd learn by now that—"

"I know, I know," she interrupted. "I'm deleting my profile. Most of the messages I get are lame anyway. All desperate, horny losers who have no idea how to talk to a woman. Ugh."

"Hey, I warned you. You should have never signed up in the first place."

"Yeah, well, you see the hours I work. Doesn't really give me many options as far as dating goes," she said as she maneuvered her way through the busy city streets.

"What have I been telling you, girl? Just date somebody here. I'm sure there's a guy good enough working right under your nose."

"Please," she scoffed. "Like who? You're the only guy there I can stomach, but you're..."

"I'm what?" he asked, sounding irritated. Not wanting to call his sexuality into question, she quickly changed the subject.

"Listen, I need to go. You know I don't like talking on the phone while driving. I just wanted to fill you in on what happened. I'll see you at work tomorrow. I'm going home to relax and hopefully enjoy my day off if I can get that idiot out of my head."

"Don't let him ruin your day, girl. Go home and pamper yourself. I have a call coming through anyway. Love you!"

She ended the call and shoved her cell phone back in her purse when it suddenly alerted her of a new text message. Knowing there was no way Doug had time to text her that fast, she glanced at the message and felt her blood boil again.

*Sorry, we got off on the wrong foot. I meant what I said about you being beautiful. Maybe we can start over? Please message me back.*

Not willing to risk an accident texting him back while driving, she tossed her phone aside and drove home every bit as upset as she had been when she left the coffee shop.

# Chapter Two
## *Mark*

Yeah, we're deleting this right now," Mark protested in a mixture of annoyance and aggravation. He'd told the woman dozens of times to stay out of his love life, but she just couldn't leave it alone.

"Just give it a chance, you big baby," Linda fired back.

"I'm not doing the dating site thing," he insisted, shaking his head angrily. "Delete it, Linda. I'm serious. Nobody can see this."

"Oh, stop. Your picture isn't even on it. I didn't even use your full name."

Linda had been his secretary since he'd opened his first *Buff n' Stuff* gym ten years earlier. Thanks to his marketing savvy, it had taken off and allowed him to open a second equally successful location, followed by a third. Within five years, he had ten locations across the state, all of them turning a fairly hefty profit. He kept membership fees low, relying on his line of accessories and supplements to generate the most revenue. Franchising had allowed him to expand exponentially, and he now boasted three hundred *Buff n' Stuff* gyms nationwide. He kept his operation running smoothly, and Linda was integral to that. Her organizational skills were second to none, and her meticulous attention to detail never ceased to impress him. Twenty-five years his senior, she'd become like a mother figure to him over the years, as his own mother had passed away when he was only fourteen. As he sat in his high-back leather office chair, Linda hovered by his side, eager to show him her handiwork.

"This is just ridiculous," he groaned as she took control of his computer's mouse and scrolled through the profile she'd created for him.

"Shush, you. Just read it."

"I'll do no such thing," he replied, crossing his arms across his chest in an act of defiance.

"Then I'll just read it for you."

She did just that, and out of respect for the time she'd spent writing it, he suffered through every word. Though he'd never dignify her by admitting it, she'd actually done an excellent job. She'd painted him as intelligent, hardworking, trustworthy, kind, caring, and funny. He liked to think he was all of those things and appreciated the affirmation. She'd left out that he ran his own highly successful company, had not mentioned his physical appearance, and had set his profile picture as a red rose.

"Well?" she asked when she finished reading what she'd written.

"I think it's a shame you wasted your time." Leaning forward in his seat, he studied the screen momentarily before asking, "How do we delete this?"

"Listen. How long have I known you now?"

"A little over a decade," he answered. She swatted his hand away from the mouse when he tried reaching for it.

"Right. And how many women have I seen you date in that time?"

"I don't know," he shrugged. "A lot?"

"Exactly. A lot."

"I'm assuming you have a point somewhere?"

"It's been a revolving door of women with you because you date these superficial bimbos who are more interested in your looks and money than who you are inside. That's a shame because who you are inside is pretty damn spectacular. You're a really great guy, Mark."

He felt himself blush at her kind words. "Thanks, Linda. That really means a lot to me."

"Don't get too excited. I wasn't finished," she smirked. "For such a smart guy, you sure are an idiot regarding women. You date these vapid floozies who can't hold your attention because they have the personality of wet cardboard."

He threw his head back and laughed at how right she was. The women in his life weren't precisely Nobel Laureates. He couldn't argue with them being mostly beauty and no brains. "You have a way with words, you know that?"

"Just look at yourself," she began, looking him up and down. "You're gorgeous. You're built like Arnold in his prime and have a face most male models would envy. You're a genetic jackpot. It's the first thing women see, and I don't blame them."

"You flatter me," he said, his cheeks flushed with mild embarrassment. She'd never talked to him this way in all the years he'd known her.

"Hell, if I were a few years younger, I'd..." she trailed off, biting her lower lip as she gave him another once-over.

"Whoa, okay, then," he blurted, playfully slapping his desk to mask his sudden discomfort. Perhaps he shouldn't view her in a motherly way after all since she was currently eyeing him lustfully. "Meeting over. Let's delete this little profile you made me and get back to work, shall we?"

"Second thing they see is you driving around in that Aston Martin of yours and know you have money," she continued, ignoring his comment. "They take one look at you in these expensive suits you're always wearing, and they're hooked. They're not interested in the real you."

"I know, I know," he said, waving his hand dismissively.

"Do you?" she asked, her brow raised questioningly. "Because you're thirty-four now, and your longest relationship, if you can even call it that, only lasted a month."

He knew she had a point but refused to concede. "I just… haven't met the right one yet."

"And you won't if you stick to the same old routine. You woo a girl with your looks and bank account and get bored with her within weeks if not days."

"Really don't know why this is your business," he grumbled, shaking his head.

"Because I care about you, Mark. I've watched you make the same mistake for the last ten years and can't keep my mouth shut anymore. You meet a girl, it fizzles out, and you mope around the office for a couple of weeks, trying to figure out what went wrong before doing it all over again. I know you want a serious relationship that these little flings you have aren't leaving you satisfied. Why not give something new a chance?"

"Oh, like this stupid dating site?" he chuckled. "I'm not socially inept. I can meet people in the real world just fine, thank you very much."

"Yeah, that's worked out really well for you," she pointed out sarcastically.

"Eh. The dating site thing just…"

"Just what?"

"It just kind of seems like it's for losers."

"Get with the times, man," she groaned. "The dating site thing is in. People meet online all the time. Perfectly normal people, I might add. People who are too busy to get out much. People who are over the whole bar and club scene. People who are new to an area and don't know anybody."

He noted the irony of a fifty-nine-year-old woman telling him to get with the times. For her age, she was surprisingly hip to the latest cultural trends.

"I don't know," he muttered as he reviewed the profile she'd created for him again.

"Listen, just give it a shot. Try it out for a week. If you don't like it, we can delete it. I made this for you for a reason, you know. With no pictures or mention of your company, a woman will be talking to you for who you really are, not what you look like and how fat your wallet is. They'll have to get to know you. The real you."

As he listened to her reasoning, he was swayed by her thinking. She'd hit the nail on the head regarding his dating life. His life had been a rinse-and-repeat cycle of superficial women who didn't care about who he was as a person. If he were being honest, he'd have to confess that he'd often lay awake at night feeling lonely, even with a beautiful woman by his side. He didn't want a trophy girlfriend; he wanted somebody who understood him and could be his life partner.

"Look, I'll think about it, okay?" he sighed, minimizing the window and pushing his keyboard tray in. "You've definitely given me something to think about."

"You promise?" she asked suspiciously. "You're not just going to delete it the second I leave?"

He laughed and rested his hands on his solid oak desk. "You have my word, Linda. I'll try it for a week, but then it's gone."

"Good answer. Meanwhile, sign the approval form for Richmond's new elliptical machine so I can send it to them. They need to get it ordered, like yesterday."

"Consider it done," he smiled as he watched her leave his office, gently shutting the door behind her.

Keeping his profile on *Plenty of Fish* minimized, he went about his work replying to emails from franchise operators and fitness equipment vendors. When he finished with his correspondence for the day, curiosity got the better of him, and he called the dating site back up. He read what Linda had written again, thankful she'd omitted any pictures and had left his username simply *"Fitness_Mark."* He knew a "mark" was a sucker, so the double meaning wasn't lost on him. He reread the profile to ensure there wasn't the slightest hint of his real identity. If any of his friends knew he was on a dating site, they'd torment him endlessly.

The website seemed straightforward enough. The navigational menu at the top listed a search option, allowing him to specify what he was looking for. He could select an age range, ethnicity, body type, height, distance, and other choices. Since he didn't plan on actually meeting anybody, he left the fields at their default settings and simply clicked "search now." He was taken aback by the overwhelming number of results and realized he may have to narrow the search a bit. After tweaking things to his liking, he searched again and was still shocked by the number of single women in the area. None of them jumped out at him, though he did attempt to read their profiles and not judge them on appearance alone. Since he was looking for somebody who wouldn't care about his looks or money, he thought it only fair that he extend the same courtesy. He knew he shouldn't be shallow if he didn't want a shallow woman.

He was ten pages deep into the search results when he realized how addictive the site was and that he'd just spent the better half an hour poring over profiles. Given his history of beautiful women, he couldn't deny that looks were important to him. He skipped anyone he didn't find physically attractive but didn't let cosmetics cloud his judgment. He knew firsthand that just because a woman is pretty, it doesn't make her interesting. With this in mind, he also skipped anyone with a weak profile, no matter how good-looking they were.

Twenty minutes later, he was fifteen pages in and still not overly impressed with any of the singles. He'd seen a few cute women who seemed intelligent, but nobody he felt he'd mesh with. He glanced at the time again and resolved to look at just one more page since it was getting late and he still needed to slam his evening workout. It wasn't like him to keep his gym partner waiting. He was a much disciplined, regimented person and tried to stick to the same daily schedule. His father was a military man who'd always driven home the importance of maintaining a routine. It had worked out for him so far, so he wasn't about to change things.

He was seconds away from giving up on the site entirely when somebody caught his eye. At the bottom of page sixteen was *"Nessa_Baby,"* a stunningly beautiful woman whose profile picture radiated a positive vibe. In it, she was wearing a purple dress and looked like she'd been caught in the middle of a laugh. Her smile was heartwarming, and her big, brown eyes seemed kind and genuine. Her profile featured three other photos as well, and she looked just as enticing in each. As impressed as he was by her beauty, he was equally impressed with what she'd written. She described herself as a go-getter with a zest for life, a career-driven woman with ambitions of someday opening her own daycare. Twenty-eight years old, she'd never been married and had no kids, though she wanted them eventually. That appealed to him since he loved spending time with his sister's two boys and had been kicking around the idea of having his own children at some point.

Her lengthy list of hobbies, interests, and passions distinguished her from the rest of the pack and showed she was much more than a pretty face. She had actual substance and appeared highly intelligent from how well her profile was written. She also came across as quite witty, a trait he'd always found endearing, and he chuckled at a few subtle jokes she'd made at the expense of the unsavory characters who'd been sending her inappropriate messages. She had spunk. That much was apparent; he seemed like somebody he'd get along with well. Still, he couldn't bring himself to pull the trigger and message her. He had a stubborn streak and didn't want to give Linda the satisfaction of knowing he'd perused the site, let alone messaged somebody. Since his profile didn't include any pictures of himself, he didn't think she'd reply anyway, and he certainly wouldn't blame her. His cursor hovered over the exit button, but he found himself unable to close out of the window. In a split-second decision, he booked her profile so he could return to it later.

After closing headquarters for the day and getting his obligatory hug goodbye from Linda, he went to the gym to throw around some weights since a strong body was just as important to him as a strong mind. He preferred to work out in the first *Buff n' Stuff* gym he'd opened a decade earlier since the place held so much sentimental value to him. His father, who had passed away two years earlier, had fronted him the money to open the gym and helped oversee its early operation. The place always reminded him of the man and, in some odd way, almost felt like home. He'd spent so much time there over the years that it had become familiar to him in a comforting way.

He thought about the woman he knew only as *"Nessa_Baby"* a few times during his workout. After showering up and heading to his spacious townhouse on the Upper East Side, he made himself his usual high-protein dinner before kicking off his shoes and sinking into his Italian leather sofa to relax with a movie.

He quickly lost interest in the cheap, predictable thriller and reached for his phone. He'd heard it sound off a few times on his drive home, but since they'd been text message alerts and not calls, he knew it probably wasn't important. As predicted, he had three new text messages from women he didn't care to hear from. He'd learned long ago not to bother replying as it only encouraged them. They were still trying to make things work with him even though he'd ended things with his tried-and-true "I think we're two different people" line. Ignoring the messages, he set his phone aside and futilely tried to finish the movie, shutting it off halfway through instead of heading to bed early.

The following work day was painfully slow. He usually kept busy replying to emails, meeting with supplement representatives, or inspecting his gyms to ensure they were kept to his standards. He'd often frequent competing fitness chains to see what, if any, mistakes they were making so he could capitalize on them. Noting where other gyms went wrong was one of the ways he'd risen to success with his own chain. Today, however, he had little slated on his agenda. As he helped Linda with some paperwork at her desk, she asked him if he'd had a chance to check out the dating site she'd set him up on. He couldn't lie to her and admitted that he had, but downplayed how long he'd spent browsing the singles.

"Message anybody?" she asked as they reviewed a franchise application.

"Nope."

"Nobody interested you even a little?"

"Give it a rest," he sighed, frustrated. "I'm not doing it. Six days, and that profile is gone."

"Do me a favor and message at least one person. If you can do that, I'll be happy."

"Do me a favor and jump off the Queensboro Bridge," he smirked.

She chuckled and poked him in the shoulder. "You wouldn't know what to do without me, buddy."

"Sadly, that's probably true."

Back in the privacy of his office, he leaned back in his chair and looked out the window at the bustling street below. So many people down there, many of them struggling to make ends meet yet going home to their loved ones at the end of the day. Money hadn't been his concern in many years, yet at the end of his day, he went home to an empty house. Two empty houses since he also owned a large home in Los

Angeles that he'd purchased five years earlier to accommodate him as he oversaw the West Coast expansion of *Buff n' Stuff*. He'd been spending his winters there to avoid New York's bitter cold and snow and didn't mind bouncing back and forth between the two locations. Regardless of what posh home he was staying in, he was still staying there alone since he hadn't met a woman worthy of a long-term commitment.

He glanced at his phone and debated calling the woman he'd met at his gym a few days earlier. She was gorgeous from head to toe and had delighted in giving him her number, but he'd been hesitant to call. She seemed nice enough, but he could tell she wasn't all that bright. He suspected he'd been pursuing the wrong women long before Linda's talk with him a day earlier. He just hadn't been able to break the pattern. He glanced at his phone again, then his computer, silently weighing his options.

Before he could change his mind, he called up the profile he'd bookmarked and began typing *"Nessa_Baby"* a message. He chose his words wisely, sending her a couple of paragraphs complimenting her profile and acknowledging her hobbies, interests, and hopes of someday opening her own daycare. He praised her drive and upbeat attitude and appreciated her humor before including a few lines about himself.

*"It's always nice, albeit rare, to stumble upon like-minded individuals,"* he told her. He went on to briefly detail his own ambitious nature, thanked her for her time, and signed his name simply as *"Mark M."* With the message sent, he pushed his keyboard tray in and returned to his view of the street below. Did he really just contact somebody through a dating site? Yes, yes, he had, but he justified it as simply appeasing Linda. Now that he'd sent a message, maybe she'd stop riding him about it and butt out of his love life again. He knew the chances of a reply were slim since a beautiful, intelligent woman probably wasn't going to gamble on a man she couldn't see. She'd likely assume he was morbidly obese, horribly disfigured, or handicapped. Still, after only fifteen minutes, he checked for a reply. Fifteen minutes later, he was checking yet again. For a man who was so quick to dismiss dating sites, he sure was eager to hear back from *"Nessa_Baby."* This fact wasn't lost on him as he anxiously awaited a response.

# Chapter Three
## *Vanessa*

Returning home from her fifth failure of a date, Vanessa drew herself a warm bath and tried to put the horrible encounter behind her. Harold's disturbing voice calling her a whore kept replaying in her mind, making the incident hard to forget. She was embarrassed that she'd resorted to a dating site in the first place since she was a very social woman and knew she was far from ugly. Since getting promoted to manager at her call center, however, her free time had all but vanished. She only had one day off a week, and that day always varied. One week, it could be a Tuesday; the next, it could be a Saturday.

Sinking into the tub, she recalled her last serious relationship and how it had ended. She'd met Daryl in a bookstore shortly after moving to New York, and he'd made quite an impression with his warm smile and inviting eyes. He was charming and charismatic, quickly winning her over with his ability to make her laugh. Things were great at first, as they always were, but problems began to arise within the first few months. He wasn't the best listener and would often interrupt one of her stories with one of his own. She suspected he tended to tune her out when she was speaking, and those suspicions were confirmed when she started asking him to repeat the last thing she'd said. She wouldn't do it all the time, just occasionally, but he never got it right. Rather, he'd stare at her blankly for a second before taking his best guess, which was always way off.

Despite their problems, she cared about him deeply enough to buy a house with him. They tried to make things work and kept it together well enough for the most part. He may have been a lousy listener, but they still got along great and rarely argued. He was such a smooth talker she could never stay mad at him, even when they did fight. He was undeniably handsome, and their sex life was decent, but things started to sour when he lost his job. He'd been working construction but was one of several employees let go after the construction company tightened their budget. To help make ends meet, she put in for a management position at her call center and wasn't too surprised when she got the promotion. She was one of their better employees, having never missed a day of work and scoring an exemplary customer satisfaction rating.

Her long hours wore away at him, and things worsened between them. While she slaved away at work, he stayed home all day with seemingly no drive to find another job. She'd gently prod him about finding work, but he'd shrug it off and feed her his "I'm working on it" line. His lack of ambition was grating since she'd always been a hard worker. Home alone all day with too much time on his hands, he began to grow restless, and his eyes began to wander. She suspected he was having an affair but couldn't prove it, and when she'd confronted him about it, he'd denied it, claiming he could never hurt her in that way. He was so convincing that she'd actually believed him, making it that much more painful when she caught him naked on their sofa with another woman. She'd forgotten an important file and had run home to get it on her lunch break, surprised to see an unfamiliar car parked in their driveway. They hadn't heard her pull up and scrambled for their clothes when she'd unexpectedly appeared, bursting into tears at the sight of them.

He didn't put up a fuss when she asked him to move out. He knew he'd messed up, and with his head hung low, he'd packed his belongings and apologized to her again before leaving her life for good. She hadn't seen him since. He'd sent her a few text messages and had left her several voicemails begging for her back, but she didn't waste her time replying. Only recently had she felt healed enough to try dating again, but with work keeping her so busy, she couldn't exactly get out to mingle. She was over the whole bar and club scene anyway, though she'd never been a huge fan and didn't have many female friends she could count on to introduce her to people. Doug was her go-to guy, but he wasn't much help as far as meeting men went. He'd been opposed to the idea of her even dating again, fearing she wasn't ready to jump back into anything, and hated the idea of her meeting guys online. Even though she wasn't thrilled with the idea, but felt she didn't have much of a choice. As much as she would have loved to cut her hours back, there was simply no way she could afford the mortgage payment working any less than she did. Online dating had seemed like the best option but had proven to be a dead end. She was hoping she might meet somebody worth her time since coming home to her two cats was beginning to get depressing. Instead, it had been a huge waste of her time.

After drying off, she wrapped the towel around herself and crawled into bed with her laptop. She had to admit the dating site was addictive. Scrolling through the profiles had provided her with hours of entertainment. She could see why most of the users were single, as they clearly had no idea how to talk to women. The majority came across as desperate, sex-starved losers who had no captivating qualities and were utterly forgettable. The men who did seem nice were, unfortunately, way too bland for her, both in appearance and personality. She rarely replied to any of her messages since they typically weren't worth replying to. They were either one or two words long, a "hello" or "hey, there," or shockingly offensive. How fun she looked like she'd be in bed was a common theme, as was how hot she would look naked. That any man thought he could get somewhere with lines like these still baffled her, but she supposed she shouldn't be surprised. The dating site was, for the most part, a collection of morons who were surely as terrible with women in real life as they were online. Most of her messages were deleted with no reply, and she'd had to block a few persistent users who weren't bright enough to realize that her lack of a response *was* a response.

Logging in, she wasn't too shocked to find fifty new messages waiting for her. Some days, she'd receive close to one hundred and wasn't sure if that was normal or not since the few friends she did have weren't members. There was a mobile version of the site she'd made the mistake of downloading but quickly deleted after the message alerts proved to be too annoying. If there was a way of silencing the alerts, she couldn't be bothered figuring it out. She opted to delete the app instead, preferring to log in solely from her laptop at the end of each workday. Knowing it was only mid-afternoon and she had the rest of the day off, she figured now would be the perfect time to delete her profile, as it seemed to be leading her nowhere fast. Since she always got a kick out of her messages, she decided to read through them before canning her account for good.

*"The things I'd like to do with that mouth,"* one of them began. *"Hit me up, and we can have a good time together."*

*"I bet you've never had oral as good as mine,"* another read.

She rolled her eyes when she got to the message asking, *"I wonder if my nine-inch cock would fit inside you? There's only one way to find out."*

Most of the others were the usual one or two words. She deleted the messages as she went along, shaking her head as she read them. She was nearing the bottom of the list when a message unlike any she'd ever received caught her attention. It was long but not rambling and composed quite well. The user, *"Fitness_Mark,"* was clearly educated and, unlike other members, had obviously taken the time to read her entire profile. That alone was enough to pique her interest. As she read his message, she found herself flattered by his appreciation for her goals, determination, and interests. He'd even picked up on the subtle jokes directed at the perverts who bombarded her inbox on a daily basis. This guy had hit all the right notes, acknowledging everything she'd written and complimenting her without going overboard. He'd sprinkled in a bit of humor that made her smile and, at one point, even laugh out loud. She was intrigued enough to check out his profile, noticing right away that his only picture was of a red rose instead of himself. She found that odd but overlooked it, noting from the information listed that he was thirty-four years old, never married, a non-smoker, had no kids, and had a muscular body type. These were all fields the website required a user to answer upon joining, but she wanted to hear about him in his own words. She scrolled down to read what he'd written about himself, which was quite a lot without being overkill. She wasn't too surprised to find it written as well as his message, and it was every bit as engaging.

Most users only bothered to write one or two short sentences about themselves, but *"Fitness_Mark"* had five full paragraphs detailing his life. He seemed to share the same drive she did, describing himself as a highly motivated man who tried to make the most out of life. As she read through his profile, she found they had a lot in common and wished he'd messaged her sooner. She read through his profile again, then returned to her inbox to read the message he'd sent her one more time. This time, his username appeared with a green dot next to it, indicating that he was currently online.

"Figures," she sighed, disappointed that somebody seemingly worthwhile had messaged her the day she'd resolved to delete her entire account. Vanessa stared at her screen for a long moment, torn between erasing her profile or messaging him back. She'd feel rude not replying since he'd put a fair amount of thought into the message he'd sent her. The polite thing to do would be to send him a quick thank you before disappearing from the site. There wouldn't be any harm in at least letting him know she appreciated his kind words. She told herself as she clicked the reply button.

*Just wanted to say thanks for the kind words. They really meant a lot to me. It was nice hearing from*

After sending the message, she stared at her screen again, conflicted. As much as she wanted to delete her profile, she was also curious what his reply, if any, would be. The site showed him as active, meaning there was a good chance he'd respond soon if he did at all. Since the only calories she'd had since breakfast had come from the cup of coffee she hadn't even finished, she chose to give him time to respond by hitting the kitchen to make herself a late lunch. She took her time, cooking for once instead of finding something quick to eat. By the time she was through, he'd replied and appeared to be online still.

*Thanks for the reply! I'm on this site under protest and will be deleting my profile soon, too. I was pressured into giving it a try and haven't been too impressed. You're the first and last person I'll be messaging. I cruised through nearly twenty pages of profiles before finding yours and was so taken by it that I just had to say something. You're definitely a breath of fresh air and have shown me that beautiful, intelligent, driven women with a ferocious wit still exist. I'm hoping to run into somebody like you in the real world someday! Then again, if my suspicions are correct, you're wholly unique, and there's nobody else like you.*

He ended the message by thanking her again for the response and included his phone number should she ever be interested. She grabbed her cell phone and programmed his number under *"POF Mark"* before making good on her resolve and deleting her profile. Reaching for her cell phone again, she shot Doug a text message she knew would make him happy:

*Deleted my profile. Done with online dating for good!*

Was she, though? She may have closed her account but hadn't been able to resist saving that guy's number before doing so. She still wasn't sure why she'd done it. Yes, he seemed like everything she was looking for, but if history was any indication, it was likely all a load of crap. He was probably five hundred pounds, unemployed, and living with his mother. That thought disheartened her. She tried not to be a judgmental person, but after Daryl, she knew she needed an honest man with ambition.

"Shit," she muttered when 5:00 pm rolled around. Her failure of a date had derailed her usual routine, leaving her with little to do, and it was far too early for bed. She normally spent her one free day a week running errands, cleaning the house when it needed it or catching up with her mother back in Georgia. She didn't feel like going back out again as she'd already washed off her make-up, her house was clean enough since she hadn't been home often enough to make a mess, and her mother was at a Christian retreat for another week. She was a deeply religious woman who always made a point of scolding Vanessa for not going to church often enough. "I don't even have time to meet a man, let alone go to church," she'd tell her God-fearing mother, to which the woman would reply, "The only man you need to meet is Jesus!"

Perhaps her mother was right. Maybe she should join a convent and become a nun. She mused as she settled into her favorite easy chair to crochet. She caught herself stealing looks at her phone and, against her better judgment, set the blanket she'd been working on aside to text *"Fitness_Mark."* She'd tried to resist, but as her mother always said, "Idle hands are the devil's workshop." She generally kept too busy to be bored, filling the spare time she did have with her many interests, but today's horrible date had made it hard to regain her usual focus. The mysterious user with no picture had also done too good of a job of rousing her curiosity.

*Hello there. It's Nessa_Baby from POF. I just deleted my profile, but I wanted to thank you again for your nice messages.*

Ten minutes went by before her phone alerted her of a new text message. Her heart sank a bit when she saw that it was just Doug replying to her text from earlier.

*Good! I'm the only man you need in your life.*

She rolled her eyes and set her phone down. Five minutes later, it sounded again, this time from her anonymous admirer.

*Six more days until I can delete mine! I promised a friend I'd keep it a week. I have no interest in messaging anybody else. Nice to hear from you! I didn't think I would.*

She smiled at his message and was quick to reply. Perhaps a little too quick, she worried. She didn't want to come across as overly eager.

*What can I say? You left an impression. Easily the best message I'd ever received there.*

*Thank you,* he replied. *I meant every word. I imagine you got a lot of messages.*

*You have no idea. My name is Vanessa, by the way. Nice to meet you.*

*Beautiful name. I'm Mark. What's going on in your world today?*

They spent the following three hours texting back and forth. He was an absolute delight as he was very easy to talk to and knew how to keep a conversation flowing. She found herself giggling more than a few times at his repartee and liked to think she'd given him a few chuckles in return. As much as she was enjoying their text exchanges, she couldn't help but wonder what his voice sounded like and daringly asked if she could call. She hoped she wasn't rushing things and was relieved by his reply.

*You know what? I'd actually love that.*

She cleared her throat and made the call. He answered on the third ring.

"Vanessa! I'm so glad you called. I was hoping I could hear your voice."

His deep, baritone voice suggested he was a bigger man, possibly carrying more than a few extra pounds, yet his username had "fitness" in it, and he had listed himself as muscular. She hoped he wasn't being disingenuous about his body type but tried to push that from her mind and focus on how easy he was to talk to.

"Right? We're on the same page there. You had me so curious!"

"You caught me at the perfect time, actually. I just got home and have some time to kill."

"Just got home from work?" she asked, hoping he'd reveal something about his job.

"The gym, actually. I try to work out at the same time every day."

If he'd been working out, perhaps he was being honest about his body type after all. "You were texting me from the gym?"

"I know, I know," he chuckled. "You texted me just as I got there. I usually have a 'no cell phone in the gym' policy. I broke my own rule for you today, so feel special."

"I do! I hope I wasn't too much of a trouble."

"Not one bit. I thoroughly enjoyed every minute of it. I can't make it a habit, though. My workout buddy was a little annoyed. But, hey, he can get over it. It's not every day I get to talk to a woman who's as beautiful as she is intelligent. That is, if the pictures were even of you." He laughed, but she could tell there was some genuine concern in his voice.

"They were really of me; no worries there," she assured him and seized the opportunity to bring up his noticeably absent photos. "And at least I had some, mister!" she teased playfully.

"Yeah, about that. My friend created the profile for me yesterday. Said they'd add photos later or something," he explained, "but there's not going to be a later because that profile is going bye-bye."

"So it really wasn't your idea?"

"What, the profile? God, no. I mean no offense. If dating sites are your thing, I'm not going to judge."

"They're definitely *not* my thing," she laughed. "Work just keeps me so busy I don't have time to get out and meet anybody. I joined that site two months ago and, well… it's been interesting, to say the least."

"Ah, so that explains it. I was wondering why a smart, attractive lady like you would resort to online dating. What do you do for work?"

"I'm the manager of a call center. How about you? I noticed your profile didn't mention anything about your job."

He laughed, picking up on her subtle concern. "Don't worry, I have a job. I'm the manager of a gym, actually."

"We're both managers. Something else we have in common."

"How do you like your job?" he asked.

"It's good, but the hours suck. I feel like I'm always working. Today's my one day off, and I spent it going on the world's worst date, if you can even call it that."

"With somebody you met from that site?"

She spent the next ten minutes recounting her meeting with Harold. He seemed smart and friendly in his messages, yet was an awkward, unkempt mess in real life. She admitted she'd made a mistake by not talking to him over the phone first. If she had, she would have realized he was a bit off and would have never agreed to meet with him. In fact, she hadn't spoken with any of her online dates before meeting them first since none of them had even seemed interested in it. It wasn't for lack of trying on her part. She'd asked all five, and all five had dismissed the idea. She wasn't sure if she was breaching some sort of online dating etiquette by even asking. She'd been new to the whole thing and didn't know what the proper procedure was.

"Jesus, I can't believe that happened to you. Nobody deserves that," he spoke after listening to her story.

"Right? Thank you. Now you understand why I deleted my profile."

"I'm lucky I caught you before you did. I can promise you that I'm nothing like that clown."

She smiled, knowing he wasn't like any of them. He was different, that much she could tell without having even seen him. Their conversation flowed so smoothly that an hour went by before either of them noticed the time. She didn't want the call to end, but it was getting late, and she had an early shift the next day. When she told him that she had to go, he politely asked if he could keep in contact with her. He was such a joy to talk to that she couldn't say no.

She woke the following morning to a text message she hoped was from Mark. She'd drifted off to sleep thinking about how charming he'd been and how good he'd made her feel. Her stomach knotted when she saw that it was from Harold.

*Please reply. I'm truly sorry about yesterday.*

"Seriously?" she groaned. She typed back:

*I accept your apology but think its best we both went our separate ways.*

Seconds later, her phone sounded. It appeared Harold had been anticipating her response. She envisioned him staring at his phone, waiting for her to message him.

*Come on. Everybody deserves a second chance.*

The guy obviously couldn't take a hint, and she was going to have to get stern with him.

*No, they don't. You had one chance with me, and you blew it.*

Another text alert sounded moments later.

*Don't be an arrogant bitch. Let's go out again.*

She felt her face getting warm as anger threatened to overcome her. Reminding herself that he was pulling her strings again in an effort to get a reaction, she gave herself a minute to cool down before responding.

*Lose my number,* she finally texted back.

*Stop. We can work through this.*

She stopped replying after that. She had to get ready for work and wasn't going to be late because of him. There was only one person she wanted to hear from today, and she hoped he wouldn't disappoint.

# Chapter Four

## *Mark*

"Seriously?" Zane asked, visibly frustrated by his workout partner's constant text messaging.

"I know, I know, I'm sorry," Mark replied, shoving his phone back into the pocket of his gym shorts.

"Ten years we've been friends now. Ten years we've been slammin' weights together, yet I've never seen you bring your phone into the gym before. You were distracted during last night's workout, and you're distracted again today. She must be something special."

"That obvious, huh?" Mark chuckled. He stepped into the squat rack and positioned himself for his next set of squats.

Zane encouraged his friend as he pumped out ten solid repetitions. When Mark had safely re-racked the bar, he asked, "So where did you meet her?"

Breathing heavily and not quite thinking straight, Mark almost let the truth slip out. "Onl—" he began, then corrected himself. "On the way home from work the other day. I had to stop by the store and run into her there."

He didn't like the thought of lying to his friend. He'd met Zane Talbot shortly after opening the gym, and the two had formed a fast bond. Zane, who sported more of an athletic build, was a successful entrepreneur heading his own lucrative marketing firm. He'd helped Mark with *Buff n' Stuff's* promotional material and had played a large role in the chain's expansion. Before meeting his wife, Zane had also been quite the ladies' man but had settled into the role of loving husband quite nicely. Mark wasn't sure if his friend had ever met women online, and it was a subject he didn't dare broach. He didn't think Zane would judge him, but he'd rather not find out.

"That's cool. I hope it works out for you. Now stop letting it fuck up our workout," Zane smiled as he unloaded a few weight plates from the bar. He was a strong guy but couldn't lift Mark's impressive weight. Despite the strength difference, the two made great workout partners. Zane was also a much disciplined person who rarely skipped the gym and always pushed Mark hard.

Near the end of their workout, Mark couldn't help but notice a very attractive woman making eyes at him from a treadmill across the gym. He tried not to look, but she was doing everything in her power to get his attention. She was a stunning blonde wearing only a sports bra and tight leggings that showed off her trim body. She smiled at him, and he immediately resented the polite nod he'd given her back. He knew she'd take the gesture as an invitation, and he wasn't wrong. Stepping down from the treadmill, she wiped her brow with her small white towel and made her way over to him.

"Looks like you have another fan," Zane joked, nudging Mark's shoulder as the blonde approached.

"Hey," she greeted her big doe eyes locked on his. She looked him over while obnoxiously chewing a piece of gum and twirling her hair.

"Hello," he returned unenthusiastically.

"I love your muscles," she said, biting her lower lip as she ran her hand down his chest.

"Thanks," he replied with a polite smile as he backed up a step. He didn't particularly like being touched by somebody he didn't know, no matter how pretty they were.

"I just joined last week," she volunteered. "I've seen you here a few times. My name's Karen."

"You're up," Zane reminded him, jerking his chin toward the squat rack. Mark could tell he was annoyed.

This wasn't the first time a woman had interrupted their workout to flirt, and he knew it wouldn't be the last. While he usually entertained their advances, today, he wasn't in the mood. He suspected Vanessa was responsible for that.

"Listen, Karen, it's nice to meet you and all, but we really need to focus on our workout."

She flashed him a look of disgust, upset that he'd dismissed her. "What are you, gay?"

"Oh, totally," he said as he moved into the squat rack. He nodded toward Zane and told her, "This is my boyfriend. Isn't he dreamy?"

"Thank you, honey bunny," Zane played along, blowing him a kiss.

The blonde replied with a long, drawn-out "wow" as she backed away from them. When she was out of earshot, Zane asked, "Okay, where's my friend Mark, and what have you done with him?"

"Shut up," Mark smirked as he unracked the bar and stepped back to his seat. When he finished, he resumed the conversation between labored breaths. "It's this girl I've been talking to, man. She's different. I really like her."

"Aw, Mark is finally growing up," Zane quipped. "I'm proud of you."

The moment the two had shared their customary fist bump, signaling the end of the workout, Mark dug his phone out of his shorts to text Vanessa back. He apologized for the delay, explaining that he had to finish his workout, and she was every bit as understanding as he knew she'd be. After their wonderful conversation the night before, he'd gone to bed feeling more fulfilled than he had in longer than he could remember. He'd sent her a text message earlier in the day and began to worry when he didn't hear back from her. He knew she worked long hours, so he tried not to get too up in his head about it. He'd breathed a sigh of relief when she'd finally texted him back.

*So glad to hear from you again! Been a busy day at work, sorry. I get out at 5:00 pm today and will hit you up then if you're free.*

*Sounds good,* he'd replied. *I look forward to it!*

Making good on her word, she'd sent him another message shortly after 5:00 pm, and they'd been texting back and forth since. He skipped his shower, knowing he could rinse off at home as he didn't want to keep her waiting. She surprised him while he was leaving the gym by asking if they could speak on the phone again, and he called her as he climbed into his car, tossing his gym back onto the passenger seat.

"Hey, you," she answered.

"Miss my voice that much?" he joked.

"I actually did."

"Really?"

"Really. You're fascinating, Fitness Mark."

He laughed at her using his ridiculous profile name. "Am I?"

"Yes. I want to know what you look like. It would be nice to put a face to that deep voice of yours."

"What if I'm really four hundred pounds?"

"I was thinking more like five hundred," she giggled, playing along.

"You're on to me."

"Hey, you never know. People can be anything they want to be online. I've learned that the hard way. You might not be the gym rat you come off as."

"I hope I don't come off that way. I don't want you to think I'm just some big meathead."

"I don't," she laughed. "I'm just teasing you."

They continued talking as he made the drive back to his townhouse. He carried the conversation inside, making a protein shake instead of an actual meal so he didn't have to interrupt their call, minus the brief sound of his blender. Heading to his study, he sunk into his armchair and listened as she opened up about her life a bit more than she had the previous night. She didn't go into too much detail, not wanting to bore him, but he hung on every word, genuinely captivated by her. He shared a little more of his own life, and her interest seemed just as sincere as he told her about his upbringing. When she asked for a recap of his love life, he left out just how many women had come and gone, simply telling her he had a history of superficial women who wanted him for all the wrong reasons. She asked him to explain, but he changed the subject skillfully.

"Oh, you know, they wanted me for my looks and my millions," he told her in a joking tone. She had no idea just how serious he was. He deflected further by adding, "I guess they just didn't do it for me. I'd get bored. I'm looking for something more."

"Like what?" she asked. "Tell me what you're looking for."

"Well," he began, "she has to be smart. That much I've learned. I can't do the dumb girl thing anymore. Not at my age. She needs to be witty since a good sense of humor is important to me. She also has to be motivated and hardworking. No more unemployed women."

That part really seemed to hit home with her. "Right? I totally get it. My ex-boyfriend didn't want to work, and it drove me nuts."

"Yeah, I need somebody independent and self-reliant. If you know where to find an intelligent, funny girl who works hard and has goals, please let me know."

"I think I know where to find one of those," she replied, and he could tell she was smiling.

They spoke for nearly two hours before calling it a night. He awoke the following morning to a text message from her thanking him for the wonderful conversation and wishing him a good day. After grabbing a quick meal, he headed into work with a spring in his step that Linda was quick to pick up on. The woman didn't miss a beat.

"My, my. Somebody's in a good mood today. Dare I ask?"

"It's not what you think," he said, rolling his eyes as he moved by her and stepped into his office.

She followed him in and studied him for a second. "Spill."

"There's nothing to spill," he replied, unable to conceal a grin that said otherwise.

Taking a seat behind his desk, he straightened his tie as he waited for his computer to boot up, purposely avoiding her uncomfortable stare. Linda was remarkably perceptive, sometimes too much so, which made keeping things from her nearly impossible.

"You met somebody," she blurted after a long moment. His incredulous chuckle revealed that she was right. "Good God, please tell me she's not another bimbo."

"She's not." He knew lying to her was pointless. He was a terrible liar anyway, and Linda was far too intuitive to put one over on.

It was her turn to roll her eyes. "You say that about all of them."

"This one's different."

"Oh? Where did you meet her? Wait; let me guess, at a stop light. She saw you in your fancy car, waved at you, and you gave her your number. Am I right?"

"Not this time," he laughed.

"At a bar? Club?"

"No and no."

"Well, I know you didn't meet her in a goddamn pumpkin patch, so just come out with it already."

He didn't want to give her the satisfaction of knowing he'd used the dating site, but he knew the truth would come out eventually. If he ever did meet Vanessa and they hit it off as well as he thought they would, he'd have to give Linda the credit. He would owe her that much.

"You know that stupid website you—"

"Shut up!" she belted. "You met her through *Plenty of Fish*?"

"Oh, God," he muttered, hanging his head and rubbing his temples. "Could you please, please keep it down? I really don't want anybody else knowing about this."

"Relax; nobody can hear us in here. Now give me all the details! I want to see her profile," she gushed, rushing behind his desk to his computer monitor. "Come on, show me!"

"You're liking this way too much, you know that?"

"Hush. Just show me."

He let out a long sigh as he called up the profile he'd bookmarked. "Tada."

She leaned closer and commented on the woman's photos. "She's very pretty."

"If they're really of her," he pointed out.

"You think she could be lying?"

"Actually… no. She sounds like a very sincere person."

"Sounds like? You've talked to her on the phone already?"

"I have," he told her. "A couple of times already."

"Wow. How did it go?"

"She's great. Her name's Vanessa. Very easy to talk to. Super smart. Funny. Nice."

"Scroll down. I want to read her profile."

Linda read over his shoulder with narrowed eyes, nodding appreciatively as she pored over every word. Mark watched her eyes scan down the page and awaited her verdict.

"Mark, this girl's a keeper," she finally spoke. "Don't screw this up."

He laughed and shook his head. "I think that's jumping the gun. She could be a total weirdo. I mean, she sounds great and all, but who knows? She could be nuts."

"I'm sure she's thinking the same thing about you," she countered.

"I'm sure she is since my profile didn't have any pictures," he returned, glaring at her playfully.

"Hey, you know why I did that. You're too handsome. She would have fallen for you before you even met in real life. Speaking of which, are there any plans to meet yet?

"We haven't gotten that far."

"What are you waiting for? Get on it before she loses interest."

He didn't think Vanessa would lose interest, but Linda's comment struck a chord. Perhaps they should hammer out a plan to meet up soon, especially since they already had such a good rapport. If she was that easy to talk to over the phone, he was sure they'd get along in real life as well.

"I'll work on it."

"And I'll work on the new franchise application we got this morning," she smiled.

"We got another one?"

"That we did. If all goes well, you might have two new locations to brag about soon," she told him as she headed out of his office. She paused at the door and turned to add, "Meet that girl!"

"Okay, okay," he laughed. The moment she closed the door, he reached for his phone.

# Chapter Five
## *Vanessa*

"You've got to be kidding me," Doug fumed.

Sitting across from him at the break room table, Vanessa felt her cheeks flush. She tried to schedule their lunch breaks together as often as she could, but today, she wasn't particularly enjoying his company.

"I knew I shouldn't have told you."

"You had five dates in a row, and all of them sucked. Do you really think this sixth one is going to be any different? You're wasting your time again."

"I'm telling you, there's something about this guy. I at least have to meet him."

"There's a reason he didn't have any pictures, Nessa. He's probably a burn victim or four hundred pounds."

"Five hundred,' she corrected.

"What?" he asked, not in on the joke.

"Never mind. Look, I almost don't even care what he looks like. He's great. If it turns out we're not compatible physically, then, hey, at the very least, I've made a friend. Lord knows I need some more."

"Sorry I'm not good enough for you," Doug scoffed.

"Stop being such a drama queen. I really like this guy. We've been talking for six days now. I can tell he's not like the others."

"Oh, wow, six whole days," he replied sarcastically, throwing his hands up.

"That's long enough for me to tell he's not a creep."

"Just cancel. It's going to end badly, and you're going to beat yourself up over it again."

She groaned in frustration and shook her head, regretting having confided in him about Mark. "I'm not canceling, Doug." Noting the time, she added, "In fact, I need to get going. It's already one, and I told him I'd be there at four."

"You must like this guy if you're dipping out early to meet him. I've never seen you blow off work."

"Mark this day on your calendar," she joked. "It'll probably be the only time it happens."

"So now, if this guy sucks, you're wasting time *and* money," Doug just had to point out.

"Yeah, well, if he sucks, I'll come back and finish my shift," she said as she stood to leave.

"I guess I'll see you back here later, then."

She laughed and rolled her eyes at how melodramatic her friend was being. "Keep your phone by your side, just in case."

"I shouldn't bail you out again, but you know I will," he sighed.

"And I love you for it," she smiled, blowing him a kiss goodbye.

Once home, she began getting ready while keeping an eye on the time. Mark had texted her to confirm that they were still on for four o'clock, and she didn't want to be late. She took a long shower, making sure she was properly washed and shaved, then spent the next hour working on her hair. She readied herself with the same painstaking effort she had with her previous five dates, choosing another sundress since it had been an unusually warm September. This one was a light pink and, like the dress she'd worn on her awful date with Harold, had a slit in the side that showed off a hint of leg. Big on matching, she chose a pink eye shadow, pink blush, and pink lipstick. She'd always been a fan of flower clips and found a pink one that matched without being gaudy. Since she didn't want to go overboard with the pink, she completed the look with a white handbag and white high heels, along with a white flower pendant attached to a silver chain that her mother had given her.

Taking a step back, she admired herself in her full-length mirror. If she were being honest, she preferred the look she'd chosen on her date with Harold but knew wearing it again so soon would be tacky. Still, she looked good and hoped Mark would approve. She lotioned up her skin to give it a more radiant sheen and gave herself one last look in the mirror.

"Work it, girl," she told her reflection confidently.

She was on her way out the door when her phone alerted her of a text message. She hoped it wasn't Mark canceling since she'd left work early and spent well over two hours getting ready. She was relieved to see that it wasn't him but annoyed to find that it was Harold… again. He'd been messaging her multiple times a day for the last six days straight. She hadn't replied, figuring he'd tire of it eventually and disappear. She kicked herself for having an older phone incapable of blocking numbers but having to cover her mortgage and the rest of the bills herself. She didn't have enough disposable income to get a new one, nor could she justify replacing a phone that was working fine. She'd never been one to care about the latest tech, and until now, her outdated phone had served her well.

*There's a new music store downtown that sells vinyl records! Want to go with me?*

"How about no?" she hissed, dropping her cell phone back into her purse and heading out the door. She made a mental note to call her service provider after her date with Mark to see if there was any way they could block his number from their end.

Fifteen minutes later, she was sitting in the same familiar coffee shop, anxiously awaiting Mark's arrival. She felt bad since it was kind of out of the way for him, but he'd agreed without complaint. It was out of the way for her, too, since she lived in Brooklyn, but this particular coffee shop held a special place in her heart. When she'd first moved to New York City ten years earlier, she'd rented a small, run-down apartment right around the corner. Because the coffee shop was so close, it had quickly become her favorite hangout. She'd explained the significance of the place to him while they were making plans to meet, and he'd seemed quite understanding.

Mark texted her to assure her that he was on his way and would be there momentarily. As she waited, her mind raced with thoughts. Her biggest concern wasn't what he would look like. It was that he had been lying to her and was really married. If he were looking to have an affair, that would explain his lack of profile picture better than any physical handicap or deformity. She remembered him telling her that his friend was going to add photos of him later, but she'd been so disgusted by the website that she hadn't gone back to check. He seemed sincere enough over the phone, but she remained cautious, reminding herself that even though he sounded convincing, she still didn't know the guy. He could have a wife and kids for all she knew.

She sat watching the door, her heart beginning to thud. She hadn't been nearly this nervous with her other dates, likely due to a complete lack of buildup—she'd spoken with them just a handful of times through written word only. With Mark, however, she'd spent almost an entire week speaking with him at length over the phone after exchanging text messages with him throughout the day. The way he spoke, with his deep, assertive voice did something to her. He knew all the right things to say at exactly the right moment.

A rather average-looking man with a slight belly walked in and smiled at her politely after having made eye contact. She was standing to greet him when he scurried by her toward the bathroom.

*False alarm,* she thought, sitting back down.

Moments later, another man walked in, and she scolded herself for hoping it wasn't him. He was extremely heavy, his clothes far too small for his obese body, and the way he was breathing didn't look healthy. She didn't want to be shallow but was relieved when he ordered his coffee and took a seat at a table across the room.

When the door opened a minute later, Vanessa stared with her mouth agape at the man who entered. Standing at least six feet tall, his muscular build stretched the tucked-in black button-up shirt he was wearing, and she could tell by how taut his gray slacks were around his thighs that he didn't skip leg day. The leather belt matching his expensive-looking leather shoes was a nice touch that wasn't lost on her.

As impressive as his physique was, his handsome face was every bit as remarkable. His angular jawline framed high, subtle cheekbones, and his baby blue eyes were kind and welcoming. He was clean-shaven, his dark hair expertly coiffed, and the smile he flashed her revealed a perfect set of teeth behind very kissable lips. He looked like a fitness model, and she saw several heads turn at the sight of him. He was the polar opposite of the man who'd entered before him, she couldn't help but note. She swallowed nervously, her mouth suddenly dry as he approached her table with his warm smile.

"You're every bit as beautiful as I thought you'd be," he greeted with an outstretched hand. She shook it and could feel how powerful yet gentle he was.

"I, well, I," she stammered, trying to form a sentence. "Wow," she finally managed, "you are *not* what I was expecting."

"May I?" he asked, motioning to the empty seat across from her.

"Of course! I'm so sorry, forgive me. I'm just a little awestruck over here."

"Oh?" he said as he sat down. "Didn't expect me to show?"

She tried to regain her senses, but his looks, combined with whatever faint cologne he was wearing, were intoxicating. It took her a moment to regain control of herself.

"I expected you to show. I just didn't expect you to look…"

"Like?" he prodded, still smiling.

"Well, like that!" she burst, gesturing to his muscular body.

"Sorry, I'm not really five hundred pounds," he chuckled. "I didn't mean to disappoint."

"No, it's not a bad thing. You're just quite handsome."

"Surprise," he grinned. "So I haven't disappointed you?"

"Not one bit." There was a brief silence, though not an uncomfortable one, as they looked each other over. "Okay, so now you *really* need to explain the whole 'no profile pictures' thing. You're gorgeous, so it doesn't make any sense that you wouldn't post at least one picture. Let me guess. You're married, right?"

He threw his head back and laughed. "Ha! I was worried you'd think that. No, no, I'm not married, I promise."

"Engaged? Girlfriend?" she prodded.

"No and no."

"So..."

"I told you my friend created the profile for me, right?"

"You did."

"My secretary, actually. Sweet woman."

"I didn't know gym managers needed a secretary."

"It's a lot more work than you'd think."

"I guess so."

"Anyhow," he continued, "she created the profile and didn't want to use any pictures of me without my permission."

She sensed there was more to the story. "That's all?"

"No," he sighed, leaning back in his seat. "She's pushing sixty. We've known each other for ten years now, and she can be a bit motherly sometimes. She said she didn't want women using me for my looks anymore." He shifted uncomfortably in his seat and looked worried that she'd find his words arrogant. He added, "Those were her words, not mine."

"I notice you said 'anymore.' I take it that's been a recurring theme. Women using you for your looks?"

"I tend to attract the superficial, yes," he shrugged. "I'm sure you know all about that. Look at you. You're stunning."

She blushed and sheepishly looked away. "Surprisingly, no."

"I find that hard to believe."

"I mean, I see men look at me sometimes, but I'm not exactly getting asked out left and right."

"They're too intimidated to ask," he told her matter-of-factly. "Guaranteed."

"So your secretary created that profile for you, hoping you'd meet a woman who'd see past your looks?" she asked, steering the conversation back to him.

"That she did. I wasn't too thrilled about it at the time. I kind of gave her an earful. It's looking like I owe her an apology since she led me here to you."

They smiled at each other for a moment, a noticeable energy between them. "Coffee?" she asked, nodding toward the counter.

"Coffee," he agreed.

She wasn't too surprised when he ordered their protein-infused java. She ordered her usual hazelnut mocha latte and didn't protest when he insisted on paying. The young barista working the counter looked them over as he rang them up. "Are you two models or something?" he asked.

"Oh, totally," Mark joked without skipping a beat. "We just finished up with a photo shoot."

"Seriously? That's awesome," the barista replied, Mark's sarcasm clearly going over his head. Vanessa covered her mouth to conceal her laughter at the boy's naiveté. She let loose her giggle as they returned to their table and found herself unable to take her eyes off of Mark as she sipped her latte.

"Well, you roped me into it, and I'm not complaining," he said.

"Roped you into what?"

"The dreaded day date," he laughed. "I don't think I've done the whole 'day date' thing in years."

"I'm sorry. It just seems safer when you're meeting somebody for the first time."

"Oh, I totally agree. I'm glad you agreed to meet me at all. Thank you," told her. "I know your other dates were a disaster, so it means a lot that you were willing to give this a shot."

"I'm glad I did," she smiled.

"I'm really not what you expected, am I?" he asked, noticing how she'd been looking at him.

"I really don't mean to stare. It's just... I still can't get over you. Smart, funny, and handsome? You're rare."

"I could say the same about you," he blushed. "Intelligent, witty, and gorgeous. Most women as beautiful as you can barely change a light bulb."

"How did you get so muscular?" Leaning closer, she asked in a whisper, "You're not on steroids, are you?"

"God, no," he laughed. "Just a lot of protein, weights, and good genetics."

"Well, I'd love to thank your mom and dad for having you," she smiled.

"If there's an afterlife, maybe you can."

"What do you…" she trailed off as she realized what he'd meant.

"My mother passed when I was fourteen. Due to Cancer. My dad just a couple of years ago due to a Heart attack."

"Oh, Mark, I'm so sorry." She was surprised he hadn't shared that with her, given the amount of time they'd spoken over the last few days.

As if reading her mind, he told her, "I didn't want to be a drag. I loved talking to you so much I didn't want to bring things down."

Conversation flowed just as wonderfully between them in person as it had over the phone. Almost two hours had gone by, their drinks long finished, when Vanessa noticed the baristas casting glances their way. She took it as their cue to get going but was so enamored with Mark that she didn't want to part ways.

"Well," she sighed, "we should probably leave before we get arrested for loitering."

"I know," he agreed, looking at the time on his Rolex watch. "What are your plans for the rest of the day? I love your company and don't want to let you go just yet."

Her heart fluttered hearing that he shared the same sentiment. "I actually have some shopping to do, but I doubt you'd want to go with me."

"You know what? I actually would."

"Really? It's boring stuff. Groceries, mostly."

"If you don't mind me tagging along, I'd love to spend some more time with you."

Her heart fluttered again. She'd never had a man want to go shopping with her before. The entire time she'd been with Daryl, they'd only gone grocery shopping together once. She'd practically had to drag him, and he'd complained the entire time.

"Are you being serious right now or just messing with me?"

"Completely serious."

"You going to put those muscles to work helping me carry in groceries?" she joked. The moment the words escaped her mouth, she realized she had just invited the man into her home. He seemed harmless enough, and her gut told her he could be trusted, but the rational part of her mind that was able to see past his good looks and charm told her to remain wary. He didn't seem like he had a temper, but if he did, he could easily snap her in half with his size and strength.

"If you want me to," he replied. "My car, your car, or should I just follow you?"

"Probably easiest if you just follow me so we don't have to drive all the way back here after. I go to the *Whole Foods* on 3rd Street in Brooklyn since it's so close to my house."

"Sounds like a plan."

He politely pushed her chair back in after she stood. She gestured for him to hold on a second and made her way to the counter to apologize to the two baristas for lingering so long. They assured her it was no big deal, but she slipped a few dollars into their tip jar anyhow. Mark held the door open for her as they headed out and made their way down the street where her car was parked.

# Chapter Six

## *Mark*

"Where are you parked?"

"That's me over there," he replied, jerking his head across the street.

"That one?" she asked, pointing at his Aston Martin.

"That's me," he answered, studying her face for a reaction.

She looked at it with a blank expression for a moment. "I wouldn't want a car that nice," she shrugged. "I'd just ding it up."

That she wasn't impressed by the car raised his eyebrows in pleasant surprise. Linda had advised him not to bring it, arguing that it would reveal his wealth and insisting that he take one of his less fancy vehicles, but he wanted to see how Vanessa responded to it. It had been a test and one she'd passed with flying colors. Most women drooled over the car that had cost him a quarter of a million dollars, but Vanessa showed little interest.

"It's an Aston Martin," he volunteered, curious if she'd ever heard the name.

"Neat," she replied rather dismissively, indicating that she hadn't. If she had, she'd know how much it was worth and would surely inquire how the manager of a nationwide chain of gyms could afford something so lavish. "Okay, just take the Manhattan Bridge down Flatbush Avenue to 3rd Avenue," she continued, unfazed by his car. "From there, take 3rd Avenue down to 3rd Street, and the *Whole Foods* is right on the corner there. You really can't miss it. Just text me if we get separated."

He knew where it was since he'd opened a *Buff n' Stuff* location near there two years earlier. Of course, he couldn't tell her that. "Sounds good."

Sinking into the leather seat of his luxury car, he followed behind her as they made their way out of Manhattan and down into Brooklyn. As he pulled into the *Whole Foods* parking lot, it occurred to him that he hadn't gone grocery shopping in years. He had all of his goods delivered directly to his townhouse every week when he was staying in New York and had them delivered to his house in California when he was staying there. He was a bit nervous to leave such a nice car parked in what appeared to be a rather suspect neighborhood but convinced himself that he was just being paranoid. Besides, Vanessa seemed worth the risk. She was everything he'd hoped she'd be and then some.

"I'm glad you were able to keep up with my sweet ride," she joked, slapping the roof of her beat-up Toyota Camry. "2002 with over two hundred thousand miles. Try not to be too jealous."

"Hey, it gets you where you need to go," he replied as he walked side-by-side with her into the supermarket. She grabbed a shopping cart and pulled a handwritten shopping list from her purse.

"So you haven't told me your last name," Vanessa pointed out as they strolled through the produce section.

"Mitchell," he heard himself say before he could stop himself. He kicked himself for lying, but Linda had driven it into his head that he should wait before revealing his true identity. She reminded him that, in an age where people carried Google around in their pockets, she could find out his net worth in seconds. He could tell by Vanessa's reaction to his car that she wasn't all about money, but he'd promised Linda he'd wait.

"Mark Mitchell," she nodded. I like it. "I'm Vanessa Claire."

"Very pretty," he smiled. "Vanessa Claire. Has a nice ring to it. I noticed your profile name was 'Nessa.' Do people call you that?"

"God, no," she laughed. "Just my mom and my gay best friend. I couldn't think of a good username, so I went with that."

He was still shocked that such a beautiful, intelligent woman had resorted to online dating, but after listening to her reasoning, he understood why. During one of their phone conversations, she'd explained to him that after kicking out her ex-boyfriend, she had to work long hours to pay her mortgage, making it nearly impossible to meet anybody out and about. With this in mind, he had to ask the obvious.

"So let me ask you something. Given how much you work, would you even have time for a relationship? You keep so busy it doesn't seem like you'd have much time to squeeze in a boyfriend."

"It would be hard, but I'd find a way to make it work," she told him. "I have one day a week off, but I know that wouldn't be enough for most guys. I've been giving serious thought to selling my house."

"Really?"

"I'm sick of living to work instead of working to live, you know? I like my job, but it's just constant. If I were to sell my house and rent something more affordable, I could cut back my hours and actually have a life."

"That makes sense."

Lying about his last name was gnawing away at him. It wasn't like him to lie, and despite Linda's best intentions, he felt she was wrong about this. Hell, she'd been wrong about the car. He'd taken it against her advice, and Vanessa didn't seem to pay it a second thought. No, if he wanted things to work out between the two of them, he couldn't start off by misleading her. He opened his mouth to speak, but she beat him to it.

"Maybe I should just hook up with a rich guy."

Her unexpected comment caught him off guard. She seemed to be joking, but he couldn't be sure. After all, she didn't exactly live in the best part of the city. Maybe she was looking for somebody with deep pockets to whisk her away from it all. He'd shown up to their date wearing eight hundred dollar Italian shoes, an authentic Rolex watch, and a car that cost more than the average home. Perhaps he hadn't done a good enough job concealing his wealth. Linda had offered to pick out a less glitzy outfit for him, yet he'd stubbornly refused and was regretting it now. His gut told him that Vanessa didn't care about money, but she was a very intelligent woman. Perhaps she was clever enough to hide her true intentions. While he hadn't known her very long, he felt he knew her well enough to trust her with the truth.

"Listen, I need to tell—"

He was interrupted by the sound of Vanessa's phone ringing.

"Crap, I'm so sorry," she said with annoyance as she fumbled around in her purse and pulled out her cell. "I forgot to put it on silent. Let me just take this real quick."

He couldn't help but overhear her tell whoever was on the other end that she was fine and that things were going great. Very great. It didn't take a genius to figure out that she was talking to a friend about their date. Since this was the second time he'd been stopped before he could get the truth out, he took it as a sign from the universe that maybe Linda was right. He'd wait a bit longer before giving Vanessa his real name and explaining his role within the *Buff n' Stuff* chain. If she was everything he hoped or she was, she'd understand and forgive the lie.

Vanessa ended the call and slid her phone back into her purse. "That was my best friend, Doug. He just wanted to make sure you hadn't hacked me up."

"Not yet," he smirked, eliciting a laugh from Vanessa.

She seemed impressed when he took over the reins of the cart and began pushing it for her. He didn't do it to score any points with her; he genuinely missed the feel of shopping, and doing it with such a beauty by his side was a whole new experience. In all the years he'd been dating, he couldn't believe he'd never gone grocery shopping with a woman. Perhaps he was simply smitten with Vanessa, but it felt oddly romantic.

They learned even more about each other as they wandered the aisles, neither of them in any rush to leave. As her shopping cart filled, she told him about her life growing up in Georgia and how she'd moved to New York City at eighteen in hopes of going to school. Life in The Big Apple was more expensive than she'd anticipated; sadly derailing her dreams, but she loved the cultural melting pot and didn't want to move back to her small hometown. She was an only child with an absentee father who'd stepped out of her life when she was only three, leaving her mother jaded and cynical when it came to men. She loved her mother dearly and kept in touch through weekly phone calls. In the ten years she'd been away from home, she'd only been able to visit twice since money had been tight. Her mother had flown to see her once, but the sprawling city had been too overwhelming for her.

She assured Mark that her story was nothing special, yet he was transfixed. His genuine interest seemed surprising to her, leading him to believe she hadn't been with the right men. He suspected they hadn't been able to see past her looks, which was something he could relate to. They seemed to have more in common than he could have imagined despite coming from completely different backgrounds.

"Uh-oh," she pretended to pout. "End of the list."

"Quick, let's grab a new cart and start again," he laughed.

After making their way through the checkout, he pushed the cart to her car and helped her load the groceries into the trunk. They lingered by her driver's side door for a moment, both hesitating to say goodbye.

"My house is right around the corner. I'd love to have you, but..."

Sensing her trepidation, he assured her, "I'm not really going to hack you up."

"I know," she giggled, playfully swatting at his chest with the lanyard attached to her car keys. "It's just… I don't know how I feel about inviting you after having just met."

"I totally understand. Don't even worry about it. I'm just thrilled I've been able to spend as much time with you today as I have."

"I haven't even had a man over in almost three years," she confessed meekly.

"Seriously?"

"Well, just Doug, but he doesn't really count," she laughed.

"Tell you what. How about I help you bring those groceries in, and then I'll scoot? I won't be an imposition, I promise. I've never been one to overstay my welcome."

He could see her debating as she chewed on her bottom lip. "Deal."

Hurrying to his car, he was relieved to find it all in one piece with seemingly no scratches. He followed her around the corner to her home, which looked a bit run down, but he didn't judge since he was raised in far worse. His father had saved every penny he'd ever earned but didn't put much of it into their modest one-story home. He recalled their porch rotting in one spot and the old man telling them to simply avoid the hole. It got even worse after his mother died. With nobody to impress, the house fell into shambles quickly, with duct tape and glue holding too many things together. It was his father's frugalness that had allowed him to open his very first *Buff n' Stuff* location, so he had no room to complain. When he ran the idea of opening a gym past his dad, a former military man who'd always emphasized a strong body, the old man had surprised him by fronting half the money. After the gym began turning a decent profit, he offered to buy his father a new house, but the stubborn Marine, then in failing health, refused to leave the comfort of the home he'd known for so many years.

Mark was able to carry six of the bags while she got the remaining two. She unlocked the front door and led him to the kitchen, where he carefully set the bags on her kitchen table. He found the inside of the house much nicer than the outside and liked her choice of decor. She was big on flowers and candles and had painted the interior in bright, pastel colors. Two cats, one black and one gray, jumped onto the table to investigate both him and the bags.

"Don't mind them," she said as she began unbagging things and placing them in the fridge.

"Do they have names?"

She paused and looked over at her two feline friends. "The gray one is Critter. The black one is Princess. I call her that for a reason. She's spoiled rotten."

"You have a nice place," Mark commented as he handed her the gallon of milk.

"Thanks," she said as she placed it in the fridge. "I painted everything myself a couple of years ago. It took me two months since I could only work on it one day a week. I just wanted to brighten the place up some. After Daryl moved out, the place just seemed… gloomy."

"You did a fantastic job."

"Thank you. You're too sweet."

"Well, I should probably get going." He'd told her he wouldn't impose and wanted to make good on his word.

Her phone sounded from her purse, this time alerting her of a text message. She looked at him apologetically. "Just one second." She fished the phone out of her purse, and he watched her face turn red as she read the message. "Mother fucker," she muttered under her breath.

He looked at her with concern. "What's wrong?"

"It's that asshole I went on a date with last week. The guy just won't give up. He texts me a few times a day. I don't reply, but he keeps texting me anyway."

"Can you block his number?"

Vanessa laughed and pointed at her phone. "Have you seen this thing? It's practically an antique."

"Call your service provider. See if they can do it."

"That's exactly what I planned on doing, actually. I'm hoping they can because I really don't want to have to waste one of my days off getting a restraining order on this guy. I swear... sometimes I feel like he's watching me."

"Want me to talk to him? I can be quite intimidating," he smiled, flexing his chest.

"You're sweet, but I got this. I don't want to suck you into my drama. Besides, I don't even know his last name or where he lives."

"Well, if there's anything I can do, don't hesitate to ask. I'm not okay with you being harassed by that idiot."

"Thank you," she smiled. "Hey, you want to stay for dinner?"

Her sudden invitation took him aback. "We've spent the last three hours together. I can't have you getting sick of me already."

"Shush. It's after seven, and all you've had is that cup of coffee. A big guy like you? I know you have to be hungry by now."

"I could eat," he laughed. "Are you sure? I love spending time with you but don't want to impose."

"Chicken?" she asked, purposely ignoring his comment.

"That works."

She gestured for him to have a seat, and he watched from the table as she made her way around the kitchen. Once again, he found himself admiring her beauty. She had hair down to the small of her back and curves in all the right places, and it was hard not to imagine her long legs wrapped around him. They spoke like old friends as she worked the oven; quickly preparing a dinner for them that was every bit as good as it smelled. It didn't go unnoticed that she'd served him extra chicken, considering his musculature. When they finished eating, he insisted on washing the dishes for her, and she didn't protest.

"This is a first," she smiled as he scrubbed their plates clean.

"Oh?"

"I don't think I've ever had a man wash dishes for me. I know Daryl certainly never did."

"Something tells me you've dated all the wrong guys," he chuckled, shaking his head.

"I'm starting to realize that."

With the dishes drying in the strainer, he toweled off his hands and thanked her again for the meal.

"Stay for a drink?" she asked, pulling a bottle of wine from the fridge. "This is the best day I've had in… well, in years. I don't want it to end yet. If you have to get going, I understand. I know you have to drive all the way back to Manhattan."

He looked at his watch and grinned, "It's only eight-thirty. I think I can stay a bit longer."

She poured them each a glass and guided him to the living room. He took a seat on the sofa and was a bit surprised when she chose to sit in the easy chair across from him instead of next to him. "I don't bite."

"Forgive me," she began apologetically. "I just... I don't sit on that thing."

"No?" he asked, looking down at the sofa in a mixture of confusion and concern. "Should I not be sitting here, either?"

"You're fine," she laughed, but her face quickly turned somber. "That's the sofa Daryl had an affair on. I came home and found him on it with some skank who lives down the street."

"Ouch," he winced.

"I haven't touched it since. I've been meaning to replace it; I just haven't had the money yet, and the room would look empty without it. I've learned just to avoid the damn thing."

"I'm sorry that happened to you. You didn't deserve that. Nobody does."

She took a long sip of her wine and changed the subject. "You've never been married? You're so handsome and charming. I'm surprised nobody tried locking you down."

He laughed and took a sip of his wine as well. "Never married." He saw a flash of skepticism in her eyes and assured her, "I'm serious. I wouldn't lie to you."

"Sorry," she said, shaking her head. "I've had some trust issues ever since Daryl."

"And I completely understand that."

He didn't have to be sitting next to her to feel the energy between them. He'd been feeling it since they first laid eyes on each other and suspected she'd been feeling it, too.

"Why are you looking at me like that?" she giggled, reacting to the flirtatious look he was giving her.

"You're just so beautiful, Vanessa. I can't get over it."

"Thank you," she blushed and nervously took another sip of her wine. "I have a confession."

"Oh?"

He felt his heartbeat quicken, worried she was going to drop a bombshell on him. She was the one who was married, or she had kids she hadn't mentioned yet. Those were the first two places his mind went. Instead, she surprised him with, "I haven't been able to take my eyes off of you all day."

He laughed, a wave of relief washing over him. "You had me scared there for a second."

"That face and that body," she said, nibbling her lower lip as she looked him over. "What gym do you go to?"

"The *Buff n' Stuff* on Parkway and East 84th Street since it's close to my place."

"Upper East Side, right?"

"You got it."

"Fancy," she nodded contemplatively.

Between his car and living in the pricey Upper East Side, he feared she'd begin questioning how he could afford his lifestyle. He hurried to change the subject. "I think *Buff n' Stuff* has a location in this area, actually. Ever been?"

"I used to go there a few days a week."

"What happened?"

"I canceled my membership after Daryl moved out. I didn't have time anymore, and the fee was a bit too high."

"I'll run that by management," he smiled, and then took another sip of his drink.

"I always thought it was a stupid name for a gym anyway," she shrugged.

He almost spit his wine out. After choking it down, he replied, "I hear the owner's dad came up with the name. It started off as a joke and stuck."

When 9:30 pm rolled around, Mark took it as his cue to get going. That was the time they'd usually wrap up their phone calls since they both worked early. She'd offered him another glass of wine, but he'd turned it down, knowing he still had to drive back to Manhattan. He wasn't much of a drinker and didn't trust himself behind the wheel with another glass in him.

She followed him outside to his car, where they hovered by the driver's side door. "I had a truly fantastic time," he told her. "Dare I say, the best date I've ever had. Remind me to give my secretary a raise."

"Thank you," she beamed. "I had a great time. You've been fantastic."

"Does this mean I can see you again?"

"Absolutely. I mean, if you can put up with my schedule…"

"I think I can manage that," he smiled. With the attraction between them almost palpable, he wrapped a strong arm around her waist and pulled her close, softly pressing his lips to hers and deepening the kiss when she didn't pull back.

"That was... wow," she blushed when their rather long kiss finally broke.

"One more," he smiled, pulling her in for another. This time, she wrapped her arms around him, feeling his powerful back as their tongues danced.

"Text me when you get home?" she breathed.

"You know I will."

# Chapter Seven
## *Vanessa*

"How are things going with steroid boy?" Doug asked her snidely, poking his head into Vanessa's office.

"Not funny," she replied, flashing him a stern look.

"Sorry, but I don't like that guy."

"You met him for, like, two seconds," Vanessa huffed, rolling her eyes.

Her bank had taken it upon themselves to refinance her mortgage, cutting her payments nearly in half. She didn't ask questions, taking it as a sign from God and loving that she'd been able to reduce her hours greatly. The free time allowed her to see Mark far more often, and things had been going wonderfully between them. A week earlier, he'd stopped by the call center to surprise her with a bouquet of daisies, knowing how much she loved flowers. His looks had turned quite a few heads, something she'd grown used to, and Doug had hurried to meet him. She could tell he was more than a little intimidated by Mark's physique and dominant stature. The man was very much an alpha male, yet he lacked the arrogance typically associated with that title. He'd been nothing but pleasant to Doug, yet her best friend still didn't approve. If Doug wasn't gay, she'd think he might be jealous of her blossoming romance with Mark.

"That was long enough," Doug, sneered, taking a seat across from her at her desk. "He waltzed in here like he owned the place, dressed to the nines and driving that showy car of his."

"His Ashton Martini?"

"It's *Aston Martin*, Nessa," he corrected, "and do you know how much those things cost?"

She shook her head, already sick of this conversation. "No, I don't, and I don't care."

"Well, I know, and I do care. It's a lot, Vanessa, a real lot. He also wears a Rolex and lives in the Upper East Side."

Mark had told her that he lived in the Upper East Side, but she wasn't exactly sure where since he still hadn't invited her over. She took him at his word and hoped he'd bring her back to his place soon since things were picking up between them.

"Are you going somewhere with this?" she asked, annoyed. "Because I have some work to finish up before I take off, and I'm sure you have a few calls to handle."

Doug threw his hands up in mock surrender. "Okay, okay. All I'm saying is there's no way a gym manager can afford that lifestyle."

"Yes, Doug, you figured it out. He's really a drug dealer." She joked, but the thought had crossed her mind.

"Hey, you never know. I'm just looking out for you, girl."

"And I appreciate that, but you can give it a rest now. I'm a big girl, and I trust the guy."

She wasn't sure how much she believed the words she'd just spoken. She'd been seeing Mark for a month now, and he seemed honest enough, yet she hadn't been able to shake the small doubt that had been nagging at her. She did want to ask him how he could afford the lavish life he seemed to be leading but thought it rude to pry into his financial situation. Things had been going so well between them; a small part of her was afraid of the truth.

After gently pushing Doug back to work, she finished up her weekly report and waved goodbye to him on the way out the door. She'd agreed to dinner with Mark at Nobu, a posh Japanese restaurant in Manhattan that he'd insisted on introducing her to. She knew the reservation had to have been pricey, yet he wouldn't take no for an answer. She ran home to get ready, dressing to impress since the famous establishment called for nothing less. The place was a celebrity hot spot, and the prospect of bumping into somebody famous excited her.

"Just a second!" she yelled when her doorbell rang five minutes before seven. Mark was always on time, which was yet another thing she appreciated about him. He let out an audible gasp when she opened the door.

"Wow. Vanessa… you look incredible."

"Do I?" she asked, pleased by his response. "I wasn't sure."

"I'm… I'm sorry, I'm still trying to catch my breath," he stammered, admiring her beauty.

With the extra money her reduced mortgage payment had allowed her to save, she was able to buy a new dress for the occasion. The red floor-length evening gown had a deep V-neck that showed off her ample cleavage while remaining classy. To change things up, she went with a sleeveless mermaid cut, and by the look on Mark's face, she'd chosen wisely. She'd bought the gown off the rack, but it hugged her body so well it almost looked tailored just for her. With money left over, she completed the outfit by picking up a pair of matching red evening gloves and a new pair of red heels. This time, she decided against a flower clip, letting her long hair fall in curls down her back.

She offered a raised hand and twirled for him when he took it. "I did well?"

"You did *very* well," he smiled. "You're missing something, though."

"Oh?" she asked, her face suddenly overcome with worry.

He reached into his suit jacket and pulled out a small velvet box. "Open it," he said, his smile widening as he handed it to her. She swallowed nervously, looking at him with unsure eyes. "Just open it," he laughed.

She slowly cracked open the box and it was her turn to gasp. "Jesus!"

"You like it?" he asked, examining her face as she took in the graduated diamond necklace.

A trembling hand covered her mouth as she continued to stare in awe at the necklace, its row of shimmering diamonds momentarily entrancing her. "Mark... It's beautiful."

"I was hoping I caught you before you put any jewelry on," he told her. "I'm glad I did."

"I can't..." Closing the box, she quickly handed it back to him. "I can't accept this. It's just too much."

"I insist. Now turn around, and let's see how it looks, shall we?"

"It's really too much. You shouldn't have." Despite her protests, she found herself turning around and lifting her hair for him to clasp the necklace around her neck. She knew she shouldn't be accepting such an exquisite gift but was so caught up in the moment that she couldn't stop herself.

"There," he said, spinning her back around to face him. He nodded in approval, as he looked her over. "Now you're ready to go out."

"Give me just a minute." She hurried to her bedroom and dug through her jewelry box for a pair of fake diamond earrings she thought might match. Luck was on her side, and they did the trick nicely. She grabbed her purse, gave herself one last look in the mirror, and quickly touched up her lipstick before returning to Mark. "Now I'm ready."

Taking her hand, he led her outside; pausing while she locked her front door, then helped her into his car.

He circled back around to the driver's side and settled in behind the steering wheel. "You're going to be the belle of the ball, baby."

"I was so wrapped up in your compliments I didn't get a chance to tell you how nice you look," she smiled. Looking at his black pinstriped suit, she asked, "Armani?"

"That's right. Custom made."

"I imagine you must have a lot of things custom-made to fit over those muscles."

"Just suits, mostly," he shrugged. "I can squeeze into most regular clothes."

She put her phone on silent so nothing could disturb their evening, and he held her hand as they drove, taking the Brooklyn Bridge into Manhattan. Nobu was every bit as elegant as she expected, oozing class and sophistication. She could see why it was a favorite among the social elite and tried not to get overwhelmed by its atmosphere. The place was packed, but they were promptly led to the table Mark had reserved for them. Always the gentleman, he pulled out her chair and waited for her to be seated before taking his place across from her.

"How can you afford all of this?" she leaned in to whisper.

"I'm a hard worker," he replied with a wink.

"You must secretly be rich."

"Oh, loaded, baby," he smiled.

She couldn't tell if he was serious and would have prodded him further if their waiter hadn't arrived with menus, successfully distracting her with the impressive, though expensive, selection of food. She'd never been a big spender, mostly since she didn't have money to spend, and wasn't thrilled with the idea of spending somebody else's money, either. When she tried to order the cheapest thing on the menu, one smelt egg for five dollars; he wasn't going to let that fly.

"No, no," he said, gesturing for their waiter to hold on. "Tonight is on me. Order anything you want."

"I am," she replied, faking a smile.

He laughed and called her bluff. "Are you? Do you even know what a smelt egg is?"

"No clue," she confessed, sharing in his laughter.

"I know you well enough now to know you wouldn't like it. Try their chicken teriyaki. That's more your style."

Speaking softly with the menu shielding her face in hopes the waiter wouldn't hear, she pointed out, "It's also thirty-five dollars."

"We won't make a habit of it. Please. I insist."

His penetrating blue eyes and charm made it almost impossible to resist him. As with the necklace, she found herself giving in despite her conscience screaming not to.

"How do you do that?" she asked after he'd placed his order for the beef tenderloin and thanked their server for his patience.

"Do what?"

"It's like you have this spell over me. I can't say no to you."

"Maybe a part of you likes being spoiled."

She hated to admit it, but she suspected he was right. She'd never had anybody treat her so lavishly. She'd been so swept away with it that she'd ignored every sign that something was amiss. The thought of him being a criminal also thrilled her, though she knew it shouldn't. The possibility of dating somebody on the wrong side of the law, perhaps a drug dealer or member of the mob, was an escape from her life that had become so mundane. She couldn't ignore it anymore. In fear of ruining their perfect dinner, she resolved to wait until they left to pry the truth out of him. If he was breaking the law in some way, as much as it would pain her, she'd have to end things between them. She couldn't allow herself to become an accomplice to whatever criminal activity he was involved in.

She pushed her concerns aside and enjoyed her dinner. She didn't spot any celebrities but wasn't disappointed. Even though she had doubts about his private affairs, Mark was the only person she cared to see. When they finished their meals, he ordered a bottle of wine that she knew had to cost a small fortune, and they shared it as they talked. As usual, he stopped himself at one glass, but she let loose and indulged with four. Like Mark, she'd never been one for the bottle but had the following day off and figured a little liquid courage wouldn't hurt if she was going to wriggle the truth out of him.

Always the gentleman, he didn't let her see the bill, but she did notice him slip their waiter what looked like a fifty-dollar bill. The wine hit her harder than she thought, and her head spun as he walked her back to the car, opening the passenger door for her and helping her in. He always opened doors for her, which was a first. Until meeting him, she didn't think that level of chivalry even existed anymore. She caught herself wondering if her mother would approve of him and shook her head to rid the thought. If Mark was a criminal, she wouldn't keep him around long enough to meet the woman. He may be gorgeous and charming, but she'd break things off in a second if she found out he was up to no good. At least, that's what she told herself. As she watched him sink into the driver's seat beside her, she realized she might already be in too deep. She was already in love with him.

"Let's get you home," he smiled, starting the car.

"Thank you for dinner. That was incredible."

"The pleasure was all mine."

With the alcohol having removed her filter, she couldn't contain herself anymore and blurted, "Are you a criminal?"

He laughed and looked at her in bemusement. "What? Where did that come from?"

"The clothes. The car. The watch. The dinner." She paused for a beat and looked at him dubiously as she added, "Your place… which I still haven't seen."

"You want to see my place? Fine. Next date, we're going back to my pad."

"Really?" she asked excitedly.

"Really," he smiled. "Want to stop by the store for another bottle of wine, or are you good?"

"I'm good," she replied. "I think I had a bit too much as it is."

"Well, let's get you home and tucked into bed."

She wanted to press him further, but the wine had done her in. Feeling her eyes get heavy, she nodded off and woke to him scooping her up in his big arms.

"Home sweet home," he chuckled, carrying her to her front porch with her purse still slung across her shoulder. He asked if she was okay to stand before carefully setting her down and steadying her with his hand on her back while she fished for her keys.

"I'm such a lightweight," she said with a touch of embarrassment as she unlocked the front door and ushered him inside.

"If you're a lightweight, I don't know what that makes me," he laughed. "You okay now?"

"I'm fine," she replied, kicking off her heels and throwing her purse on the counter.

"I'm glad you had a good time. Mission accomplished."

The attraction between them had been slowly rising to a fever pitch. Four weeks they'd been seeing each other, yet they'd never taken things beyond impassioned kisses. She'd wanted to take things slow, something he was fine with, but it was becoming increasingly difficult. She'd lay awake at night wondering what he looked like underneath his clothes, touching herself at the thought of him ravaging her body. Aesthetically, he was her definition of the perfect man. However, there was much more to him than a gorgeous face and incredible physique. He treated her better than any man ever had, making her feel special every single day.

She swallowed nervously as he closed the distance between them and pulled her into his arms. He looked exceptionally striking in his expensive suit, and the wafting scent of his subtle cologne always did something for her. She wasn't sure if it was the wine or the look of arousal in his eyes that was making her feel so intoxicated. He wanted her, and despite the voice of reason telling her to wait until she found out his real story, she wanted him, too. She hadn't been touched by a man in nearly three years, and her body ached to feel him. Taking him by the hand, she guided him down the hallway into her bedroom.

"Help me out of this thing," she smiled, turning around and throwing her hair to the side so he could reach the gown's zipper. Getting the thing up all by herself had been a big enough pain. She wasn't going to turn down the chance to have him help her out of it.

"You're not still drunk, are you?"

She wasn't sure if he was joking or trying not to take advantage of her. "No, silly. Now come on."

She didn't have to tell him twice. He gently pulled the zipper down, and she felt his eyes on her backside as she stepped out of her heels and tugged the dress off. Turning around, she searched his face as she stood before him in her bra and panties and felt a sense of relief when she saw exhilaration instead of disappointment. She wasn't stupid and knew he'd been with his fair share of beautiful women. She'd worried she wouldn't compare to his previous conquests, but his words quickly put her at ease.

"Vanessa... you're gorgeous."

She smiled but said nothing, pressing her body to his and looking up at him with her big, brown eyes while she unbuttoned his suit jacket. Following her lead, he shrugged it off and let it fall to the floor, then tugged his tie loose as she began to unbutton his shirt. She slowly peeled it off his broad shoulders and tossed it aside to admire his musculature.

"Holy shit," she murmured. She could see the striations in his bulging chest, oblique's, his abs, unlike anything she'd ever seen. His body was even better than she'd spent so many nights imagining.

She shut off the light and took his hand again, leading him toward the bed. With the bedroom door open, the light from the hallway provided all the ambiance she needed. She could still see his body and the lustful look in his eyes as he wrapped a powerful arm around her waist. He leaned in to kiss her; their tongues mingling as his free hand expertly unclasped her bra. When it dropped to the floor, she took it as her signal to finish undressing him and unbuckled his belt to gain entry to his pants. She unbuttoned them while he kicked his shoes off, their lips still locked in a fevered kiss as she pulled his zipper down. He took over from there, stepping out of his pants and brushing them out of the way with his foot. After making short work of his socks and throwing them into the growing pile of clothes, he stood wearing only his black boxer briefs. She took a step back and soaked in his body again, this time noting his pronounced leg muscles. She saw his eyes drift down to her bare breasts, and the look of desire on his face told her he approved. The growing bulge in his boxer briefs reaffirmed that approval. Biting her lower lip, a habit she wasn't aware she had until meeting him, she stepped toward him and ran her hands over his massive chest, then down his abs to the waistband of his underwear. She'd always heard that muscular men were often overcompensating for a shortcoming in their pants. This certainly wasn't the case with Mark. Pulling his boxer briefs down, she was greeted by his impressive cock that was standing at full attention.

"Wow," she gasped, looking down at it. She took it in her hand and began to stroke him as their lips reconnected.

"I want you," he breathed, gently pushing her down onto the bed and stripping her panties off. She'd suspected this might happen and thanked herself for having shaved.

He was careful not to crush her as he climbed on top of her, supporting himself with his imposing arms. She purred as he began kissing her neck, loving the feeling of his lips on her skin. He made his way down to her breasts, covering them with kisses before cupping one in his big hand and taking a hard nipple in his mouth. He gently sucked and nibbled it as his other hand slipped between her legs, and she moaned as he slid one of his thick fingers inside of her. She would have been embarrassed by how wet she was if he didn't seem to love it so much.

"Fuck, that's so hot," he said, slowly backing his finger out of her. It was slick with her juices, and she watched as he licked it clean. "You taste amazing."

"Yeah?" she asked softly.

"I want more. I want you all over me," he replied gruffly, trailing kisses down her body.

She writhed when he slipped his finger back inside of her and moved between her legs, kissing her inner thighs. He teased her by taking his time, building her anticipation as he kissed his way toward her swollen clit. When he flicked his tongue against it, her back arched, and she moaned loudly, running her fingers through his hair.

"You like that, baby?" he smiled up at her devilishly. Before she could reply, he ran his tongue up the length of her pink slit, causing her to cry out in pleasure. He did it again, eliciting the same response. She could see the large, defined muscles of his right arm working as he slid his finger in and out of her while skillfully licking and sucking her clit.

"Oh my God," she murmured, her voice trembling. She grabbed at the blanket with one hand, fisting it tightly, while the other squeezed his shoulder. "Oh, my God," she repeated. "Oh my fucking God!"

"That's it, baby." He paused to place her hands on the back of his head and looked up at her assertively. "I want you to fuck my mouth."

She'd never had anyone talk to her in such a way, and she had to admit… she liked it. He was a man who knew what he wanted and wasn't afraid to ask. Holding the back of his head, she guided him as he mouthed her eagerly. Under normal circumstances, she wasn't a fan of having this done… but nothing about Mark was normal. Whereas most men were terrible at it or looked like they hated it, Mark was incredible and genuinely loved every second. She let him up for air and could see how wet his chin was. She'd never reached climax through oral before, but that changed when she pushed Mark's head back down. The combination of his expert tongue and finger pushed her over the edge, and she exploded in his mouth, shaking as the orgasm rocked her body.

"Oh, fuck," she panted, her chest heaving as she rode out the aftershocks.

"I love the way you taste," Mark said, wiping his glistening chin with the side of his hand and licking it. He kissed his way back up her body, stopping to enjoy her breasts again. She welcomed his mouth on them while she recovered from the intense climax, and when she had control over herself, she reached down for his cock, feeling it get hard again in her hand. While his mouth and hand had been great, she needed more. She wanted him inside of her but worried he wouldn't fit.

"Easy," she whispered as he positioned his hips between her spread legs.

He grabbed the base of his shaft and carefully guided his tip into her wet slit, then worked in the rest of his thick member. He filled her completely, and discomfort turned to pleasure after stretching to accommodate his size.

"Yes, just like that," she breathed as he slowly pumped himself in and out of her. She wrapped her legs around him, her hands holding onto his muscular arms as he began to thrust into her faster. She looked at her fingers gripping him and marveled at the way his pale complexion contrasted against her chocolate skin.

"God, you feel so good," he moaned. "Take this dick, baby."

She was never this vocal in bed but found herself feeding off of Mark's energy. She heard herself saying things she never dreamed she'd say. "Give me that big cock. Don't stop. Give it to me, baby. That's it."

She couldn't believe the words escaping her mouth, yet she couldn't stop them from sounding as Mark did what she asked, ramming himself into her harder and faster. He came to an abrupt stop and, as if she weighed nothing, flipped her over to take her from behind. She lifted her ass for him and lowered her upper body, sinking her head into the pillow as he entered her again. She used the pillow to stifle her cries as another powerful orgasm surged through her, followed by another. He'd made her climax twice in a row, which was something she never thought possible.

She heard his coital grunts and groans getting louder as he gave it to her even harder and knew he was getting close. "Do it, baby. I want it all. Give it to me. I want every drop."

Again, she was taken aback by her own words. She knew she wasn't on birth control and should have at least insisted on a condom, yet her arousal had clouded her better judgment. At that moment, all she wanted was for him to drain himself inside of her. He did just that, squeezing her ass as he pumped her faster until he released an almost pained groan. Looking over her shoulder, she watched his muscles contract and his face twist as he filled her with his cum. He collapsed next to her, breathing hard and his body gleaming with a thin layer of sweat.

"V-Vanessa," he stammered as he fought to regain his wind. She watched his chest moving up and down, still in fascination with his muscularity. "That… that was amazing."

"I know," she smiled, cuddling up next to him. He wrapped an arm around her and held her as she softly ran her fingers over his chest. "Three times."

"Three times?" he asked, looking puzzled.

"That's how many times I came, silly," she smirked, playfully swatting his shoulder. "I usually don't even cum once."

"I'm flattered," he chuckled, still catching his breath.

She could see beads of sweat on his forehead and joked, "At least you got some cardio in today, huh?"

"Oh, don't think I'm done," he grinned. "I just need a second to recover."

She felt her body tingle at his words. The sex had been so good she wouldn't turn down another round, but she needed a moment to recover, too. As her fingers explored his body, she asked quietly, "You're not a drug dealer?"

"No," he laughed. "You're still on that?"

"Are you… in the mob?"

"Just listen to yourself," he laughed again, shaking his head. "You watch too many movies."

"Well, you never explained…"

"I will," he assured her, gently kissing her forehead. "I promise. I'll bring you over to my place and explain everything. But right now," he rolled on top of her and looked at her with his blue eyes renewed with lust, "right now I want to make love to you."

She swallowed hard, her heart beginning to thud. "Make love? Is that what you call what we just did?"

"No. That was a good fuck. A *really* good fuck. We both needed to get it out of our system. I know you've wanted me as badly as I've wanted you. But now… now I want to make love to you."

She reached up and gently traced his lips with her thumb. "Are you in love with me?"

"I am," he nodded. She searched his eyes and knew he was sincere. "I've been in love with you since the moment I laid eyes on you in that coffee shop. You're everything to me."

Her eyes welled with tears. With trembling lips, she told him, "I love you, too. So much. Please don't hurt me."

"I won't, baby."

He kissed her forehead again, and, in another first, she experienced what it was to make love for the first time.

# Chapter Eight

## *Mark*

"Mark! Mark, wake up." Vanessa's alarmed voice woke him from his sleep.

"I'm up, I'm up," he groaned, rubbing his eyes. "What's going on? Are you okay?"

She sat on the bed next to him with her cell phone in her hand. She was visibly shaken and looked like she was about to burst into tears. "It's Harold. He has texted me again."

"What?" he asked groggily, still coming to his senses. "I thought you managed to get him blocked?"

"I did! It looks like he finally caught on and got a new number."

She handed him her phone so he could read the text message that read:

*Nobu. Fancy. You should have given me a chance. I would have taken you.*

"Jesus, this guy really is a creep," Mark said, sitting up in bed next to her.

"Look at the time he sent it. Eight thirty last night. That means he was there, Mark. He was watching us.

I had my phone on silent and didn't even see the message until now."

"Yeah, I hate to say it, but it might be restraining order time. He's clearly unhinged."

"How can I get one, though? I don't know his last name or where he lives. I think the authorities need that stuff. Hell, 'Harold' might not even be his real name."

"I doubt anybody would make up the name 'Harold,'" Mark pointed out. "Let me text him back. Maybe that will scare him off."

She passed him her phone, and he replied:

*Hi, Harry. This is Vanessa's boyfriend. I suggest you leave her alone unless you want your face rearranged.*

"There, problem solved," he smiled, giving the phone back to her.

"You're the best," she beamed, leaning over to kiss him. "After seeing the size of you, I'm sure that message just scared the piss out of him. He'd have to be a complete idiot to—"

Her phone alerted her to a text message, interrupting her thought.

*Enjoy her while she lasts, tough guy. She won't be yours long.*

"Are you fucking kidding me?" she spat, throwing her phone down on the bed in anger. Mark picked it up and read the message.

"Wow. Yeah, I'd say its restraining order time."

"Awesome. This is just how I wanted to spend my day off."

"Let's just get it over and done with," Mark said, rubbing her back in an attempt to calm her down. "We'll go now and get it taken care of."

"We? Baby, don't you have to work today?" She paused, realizing she still wasn't entirely sure what he did for work. She let it go and continued, "I'm not about to have you miss work over something I got myself into."

"Hush. I set my own hours. There's no way I'm having you go through this alone. I got you."

"Are you sure?"

"I wouldn't have it any other way."

As she took a quick shower, he grabbed his cell phone from his suit pants that were still inside out on the floor. He texted Linda to let her know he'd be coming in late and she returned his text moments later asking if he was okay. Her concern was warranted as he was never late for work, but he was quick to assure her that he was fine.

He knocked on the bathroom door and asked Vanessa if he could join her to save time. She happily invited him in, and he was surprised to find the water temperature to his liking. Most women seemed to take blisteringly hot showers that made joining them impossible, but not Vanessa. Yet another thing to love about her, he mused as he washed her back. She returned the favor by washing his as he let the warm water wash away their incredible sex. She got out first, allowing him to finish up while she dried off. She handed him a towel when he was through, and he joined her back in her bedroom.

"I hope this crap with Harold doesn't spoil your memory of last night," he told her as he slid his boxer briefs back on.

"Baby, *nothing* could spoil that memory," she smiled, cozying up next to him, wearing only the towel wrapped around her body. "It was amazing."

He pulled her closer to him and kissed her deeply while hooking his fingers on her towel and pulling it loose. It fell to the floor around her ankles, and he took a step back, looking over her naked body for a moment. "Goddamn, you're sexy."

"I'm glad you think so," she smiled, moving toward him again and cupping the growing bulge in his boxer briefs. "And I'm glad he thinks so, too."

"Oh, he definitely thinks so," he breathed as she began to stroke his cock through the fabric of his underwear.

"That feels good, baby?" she whispered in his ear.

"You have no idea," he moaned, his eyes closed as he enjoyed her hand working his shaft.

"I want to taste you," she said, unexpectedly dropping to her knees in front of him. Pulling his thick cock from his boxer briefs, she looked up at him with big, innocent eyes. "Can I?"

"F-fuck yes," he stammered, looking down at her.

She shot him a mischievous smile as she flicked her tongue against his tip.

"You little tease," he smirked.

"Is this what you want?" she asked. Before he could answer, she took him in her mouth, running her hand up and down his shaft as she sucked him. He gripped her shoulder with one hand, the other resting on his hip as he watched her work.

"That's so fucking hot," he groaned, his hips beginning to thrust as she continued pleasing him.

She wasn't able to talk with his hard cock in her mouth but let out a stifled "mmm" as she took him deeper until she gagged.

"Easy, baby," he breathed. "I don't want to choke you."

She looked up at him again, and the sight of her pretty face with his cock in her mouth was almost enough to push him over the edge. Her hand glided along his shaft harder and faster as she picked up the pace, sensing that he was getting close.

"Oh, fuck!" he groaned, unable to hold out any longer. She pulled his cock out of her mouth and jerked him off, watching as he shot his cum all over her bare breasts.

"That's it, give me every drop," she whispered, continuing to stroke him until he'd emptied himself completely. She looked down at her chest, now dripping with his rather large load. "Jesus, that was a lot."

"S-sorry about that," he grinned. "Take it as a compliment."

"Next time, remind me to do that before I take a shower," she laughed. Picking her towel up from the floor, she used it to wipe herself clean and threw it in the hamper by her closet door.

"You're incredible, you know that?"

Forty-five minutes later, they were in Kings County Criminal Court and an hour after that, they were in front of a judge who was of little help. Vanessa had deleted all of the harassing messages from Harold's original number, and the two texts from his new number weren't menacing enough to necessitate an Order of Protection. Since she didn't even know Harold's last name, there wasn't much the court could do anyway. The judge advised her to save every text message from the new number and to call the police if they got threatening enough. If Harold's behavior escalated, the cops might be able to arrest him for stalking.

"Well, that was a waste of time," Vanessa muttered once they'd left the courtroom.

"I kind of saw it going that way," Mark sighed. "Just not enough to go on yet."

She took his hand and smiled up at him. "Thank you for coming. It really means a lot to me."

"I always got your back," he told her. He brushed her cheek with his thumb and kissed her gently. "I need to run home and get changed. I'd rather not go to work in a wrinkled Armani suit."

"I should have ironed it for you before we left. I'm sorry."

"I think you had other things to worry about," he laughed. "Besides, I live close to the gym. It's not like it's out of the way."

After dropping her off at her house and kissing her goodbye, he drove back to the Upper East Side and was surprised to find his sister's car parked outside his townhouse. He'd given her a key and told her she was welcome to let herself in anytime, night or day, but she'd never taken him up on it before. Inside, he found her on his sofa watching television with her two boys.

"Uncle Mark!" the kids screamed in happiness, running over to him with their arms outstretched. He bent over and scooped them up, one in each arm.

"There are my two favorite guys!" he smiled, bouncing them up and down as they laughed.

"I texted and called you, but you didn't reply," his sister said, looking at him apologetically.

"I'm sorry. I was in court and had my phone on silent. I haven't checked it since."

"You were in court?" she asked, looking at him with concern.

"Relax," he told her as he continued bouncing his cackling nephews around. "I just had to help my girlfriend out with something."

"Girlfriend? Man, I've missed a lot."

Shannon, four years his junior, had made a name for herself as a respected defense attorney. She shared his work ethic and had always excelled at everything she put her mind to. When she announced at seventeen that she wanted to pursue a career in law, he didn't doubt for a second that she'd do it. Unlike Mark, however, she'd already settled down, marrying a partner at her law firm six years earlier. Her two young boys—now three and five—always put a smile on his face. James and Bradley were always overjoyed to see him as well and seemed to love using him as their human playground.

"I think you've gotten even bigger!" James giggled, hanging from his uncle's forearm.

"Okay, boys," Mark laughed, shaking the two off of him. "Do me a favor and watch television for a few. I need to talk to your mom."

"But—" they began to protest, only to be interrupted by their mother.

"Listen to your uncle," Shannon told them sternly. "You can play with him in just a bit, I promise."

Defeated, the two boys took a seat in front of the television. Looking at his sister, Mark jerked his head to the kitchen, and she nodded her understanding. She followed him to the kitchen table, where he pulled out a chair for her and motioned for her to have a seat.

"What's going on?" he asked, safely out of earshot from the boys. "Is everything okay?"

"I'm so sorry to barge in on you like this. I just needed to get away and didn't know where else to go."

"It's never a problem, really. You know you're always welcome here. What happened?"

"Travis and I got in a huge fight this morning. I found out he's been having an affair."

Mark wasn't too shocked by this news. He'd met her husband a handful of times and always got a bad vibe from the guy. "Jesus, I'm so sorry. Are you sure?"

"Positive. I found the messages between them. For a smart guy, he sure is stupid. He didn't realize his tablet was linked to his phone. I took the boys and left. I was hoping we could stay here until I figure out what I'm going to do."

She looked at him pleadingly, and he took her hand in his. She'd always been a strong woman, but he could see her fighting back her emotions. "You can stay as long as you want. I'd love to have you and the boys. Take all the time you need. My place is yours."

"Thank you," she said, her lower lip trembling as she came undone. She sprang into his arms, and he embraced her, patting her back while she cried.

"There, there," he told her softly. "It's okay. Let it all out. You know I'm always here for you."

"You're the best," she sniffled, pulling back and wiping away her tears with her sleeve.

"Listen, I'm supposed to be heading into work, but I can take the day off if you need me."

"Nonsense. You have a big, important company to run. I'll be fine."

"You sure? I really don't mind…"

"I'm sure," she smiled. "Now, tell me about this girlfriend of yours before you run out the door."

Mark was more than happy to fill her in on his new relationship, and his sister seemed genuinely happy for him. For years, she'd been pulling for him to meet the right girl and settle down. After gushing about Vanessa, he spent some time with his nephews before changing into a less formal, less expensive suit. When Shannon and the boys followed him out to the car to see him off to work, the moment pulled at his heartstrings, making him wish he had children of his own.

He could tell his sister was hurting deeply. He pulled her in for a long hug, and then brushed a wave of hair from her face so he could kiss her cheek. "I love you."

"I love you, too," she replied, choking back another round of tears.

Kneeling, he hugged the boys and assured them they'd play when he got home from work. He made a mental note to pick up a few toys on his way home as his bachelor pad wasn't very kid-friendly. As long as they were staying with him, he was going to make their time there as comfortable as possible, even if it meant spoiling them rotten.

# Chapter Nine

## *Vanessa*

It had been a week, yet Mark still hadn't made good on his word. He hadn't brought her to his place, and he hadn't disclosed anything more about his life. She'd stopped asking, hoping he'd tell her when he was ready. She had to confess. A part of her still didn't want to know. Things had been incredible between them, and she feared the truth would ruin it all. She'd also been distracted by more texts from Harold, all of them annoying but none of them harassing or threatening enough to involve the police. She suspected if she blocked his number again, he'd message her from a new one, so she chose to wait it out. She was going to save every text he sent until he crossed the line and she was able to report him.

"Gee, thanks for finally making time for me," Doug remarked critically as he let her in. Movie night had been their monthly ritual for almost three years, but she'd been so preoccupied with Mark that she hadn't been making time for it. After one too many passive-aggressive comments at work, she finally set aside a night just for Doug. She felt awful for neglecting their friendship, and Doug wasn't being very forgiving. *The way this guy holds onto things, you'd think he was a woman,* she'd thought to herself on the drive over.

"I know, I know. I'm sorry," she replied as she made her way inside his small Brooklyn home. "I've missed this, I really have."

"Sure," he scoffed as they moved into the kitchen. "I know you're only here because he's out of town."

"That's not true," she shot back. She hoped she'd sounded more sincere than she felt. If Mark hadn't been called away to a training seminar, she probably wouldn't be here with Doug. She'd be with Mark, having her mind and body rocked as they made love again. Still, Doug didn't need to know that.

"I'm not an idiot, Nessa," he sighed, rolling his eyes. She wished she'd never told him about Mark leaving.

"Shut up and throw those Pizza Rolls in the oven, you big baby," she laughed. "I need snacks and some quality time with my best friend."

His sour look melted away, and he cracked a smile. "You know I can never stay mad at you, girl."

"There's the Doug I know and love," she smiled back as he pulled the bag from the freezer.

With the oven preheating, they headed into his living room and seated themselves on his ugly yet comfortable plaid sofa. It had become quite familiar to her since it was the only sofa she'd sat on in nearly three years. Doug knew why she refused to sit on hers and had offered to trade, but neither of them had a truck. At least, that was the excuse she'd given him. The reality was, as comfortable as his sofa was, it was a complete eyesore, and she didn't want it in her house.

Doug's place was quite small and in rather poor shape. She knew most gay men prided themselves in appearance, but the call center didn't pay him enough to improve the old house that he'd inherited from his mother. She didn't mind since it had offered her a nice escape from her place over the years and given her a break from her lonely nights at home.

His two cats, Cocoa and Pebbles, joined them on the sofa to rub up on her. She pet them as she listened to Doug complain about his recent calls at work. She had his job before she got promoted, so she understood the need to vent and didn't mind lending an ear. When the oven beeped, signaling it was finally preheated, Doug hurried to the kitchen and returned seconds later, announcing that the Pizza Rolls would be ready in ten minutes. The snacks differed every time and were usually something they'd both agreed to beforehand. It was a fun tradition they'd established, one that was uniquely theirs and generally something she looked forward to. Tonight, however, it felt forced. Her mind kept drifting to thoughts of Mark, but she tried not to let it show and did her best to keep her phone at a distance. She'd managed to snap Doug out of his mood and didn't want to trigger him again by texting Mark all night.

With their snacks fresh out of the oven and cold cans of soda by their side, they snuggled up under his plush blanket to escape the real world together. Doug had picked out the movie, which she was fine with since he usually had decent taste. Tonight's choice was noticeably darker than usual, but she still enjoyed it and was proud of herself for making it through the entire thing without checking her phone. The moment it was over, though, she rushed to see if Mark had messaged her.

"Anything from steroid boy?" Doug asked bitterly.

"Stop. He's a good guy."

"Sure. Have you seen his place yet?"

"We're… we're working on it."

He laughed and shook his head. "That's what I thought."

She felt herself getting heated. Not because she was mad at him but because she knew he was right. There was no excuse for not having seen Mark's place yet. He'd been purposely keeping it from her, and she'd foolishly allowed it in fear of what she might find. Drugs, guns… she wasn't sure but knew it wouldn't be good. He seemed to have too much money to be a simple gym manager.

"I know," she replied somberly. "It's hard, Doug. I know he's probably hiding something, but… I love him."

"Whoa, wait, what?" Doug bolted upright with his brow raised in alarm. "You *love* him?"

"Yes. And he loves me, too."

"You've got to be fucking kidding me. I thought this was just some little fling you were having. I didn't know you two were this serious."

"I should have never let things get so far," she sighed. "I just couldn't stop myself."

He looked at her skeptically. "Do you *really* think he's at some training seminar?"

She took a moment to think it over and shrugged, "I don't know. I want to believe him, but he could be doing anything right now."

"Text him and ask," Doug suggested. "I'm going pee."

He threw the blanket aside and made his way to the bathroom, leaving her alone with her phone. She wasn't surprised that Mark hadn't messaged her since she'd told him earlier in the day that she'd be watching a movie with Doug. Knowing how considerate he was, he probably didn't want to interrupt. She didn't want to accuse him of anything, so she chose a more subtle approach, texting him:

*Movie over! Hope your night is going well... wherever you are.*

She had just set her phone down when her text message alert sounded, immediately followed by another and yet another. Mark rarely sent her more than one message at a time, so the string of texts alarmed her. Picking her phone back up, she was dismayed to find that all three were from Harold, not Mark. She would have ignored them had Doug not been in the bathroom. With a moment to spare, she decided to see if he'd finally said something incriminating. The first message read:

*Mark Masterson sure has a fancy townhouse.*

She moved on to the second message reading:

*That he shares with his beautiful wife and two kids, she's a hotshot attorney. No wonder he can afford such nice things.*

The third message contained no text, only a short video. Her heart pounded, and her jaw clenched as she played it. She covered her mouth in shock at the sight of Mark tenderly kissing a woman on the cheek and mouthing the words "I love you" before bending down to hug two little boys. She turned her phone's volume up all the way and replayed the video. This time, she could not only see him say the words, but she could faintly hear them as well. More damning, she could hear the woman tell him that she loved him, too. She replayed the video again, her hands shaking as she watched Mark with his wife and kids.

*"Doug! Doug!"* she screamed, beginning to hyperventilate.

The toilet flushed, and Doug bolted out of the bathroom with a look of concern, still zipping up his pants as he quickly made his way to her side. "What is it? What's going on?"

Barely able to speak, she dropped her phone onto the sofa next to him and pointed at it with a shaky hand. "T-t-the v-video," she stammered. "W-w-watch the v-v-video."

He rubbed her back to calm her while picking up the phone with his free hand and playing the video. He watched with wide, unbelieving eyes, and then replayed it again to make sure he'd seen and heard what he thought he had. "Oh, Jesus. Vanessa, I'm so sorry."

*"Fuck!"* she yelled, punching the wooden coffee table in front of them. Her empty soda can flew onto the floor, and the spooked cats scurried off to hide. *"I'm so fucking stupid!"*

"There, there," Doug spoke comfortingly, continuing to rub her back. "I told you something was up with that guy."

"He's married. I can't believe it." Overcome with emotion, she began to sob as a mixture of disappointment, anger, and heartbreak flooded her. "He's married and has kids, Doug."

"That's it, let it all out," he said in a soothing tone as he wrapped his arms around her and pulled her close. "I'm here for you. We'll get you through this."

"Mitchell isn't even his last name!" she cried, her tears spilling down her cheeks and onto Doug's shirt. "He lied to me about everything. Everything!"

Pulling back from Doug's hug, she wiped the tears from her face and reached for her phone. She began to search the internet while Doug looked at her in confusion. "Nessa, what are you doing?"

"Getting the number for his gym," she sniffled.

"Uh, why? I'm pretty sure they're closed now anyway."

She shook her head. "No. It's a twenty-four-hour gym with a staff member always there. That's one of their big selling points. You've probably seen the commercial."

"Do I look like I care about gym commercials?" Doug chuckled, looking somewhat embarrassed as he pointed at his belly.

She put her phone on speaker and held up her index finger, gesturing for him to be silent as she spoke with the employee who'd answered. "Yes, hello. I was wondering if it would be possible to speak with Mark Mitchell, please."

"I'm sorry, who?"

"Mark Mitchell," she repeated. "I believe he's the manager of that location."

"I'm sorry, but there's no Mark Mitchell here," the employee told her. "Our manager's name is Greg Simmons. He should be in around eight in the morning if you want to speak to him."

"Thank you," Vanessa said her voice cracking as she began to sob again. She ended the call and threw her phone aside, then buried her face in her hands. "So dumb. I'm so dumb."

"No, you're not," Doug assured her. "We all make mistakes."

He coaxed her back into his arms and held her as she wept. When her tears began to lessen, he handed her one of the napkins from the coffee table. She used it to dry her face and let out a long, heavy sigh. "This explains everything."

"It really does," he agreed, one arm still wrapped around her.

"The expensive clothes, the fancy car, the townhouse… his wife probably paid for half of it." She thought for a moment and laughed in disgust, "She probably paid for half of that necklace he gave me, too."

"He gave you a necklace?"

She wiped away more tears and ran her hand through her hair. "Yeah. I knew I shouldn't have accepted it. It was all too good to be true. Here, I thought he was a criminal or something. Turns out he's married, and, somehow, that actually seems worse."

"His poor wife and kids," Doug muttered, shaking his head.

"Right? And who knows what he really does for work," she said, throwing up her hands. "He certainly doesn't work at that goddamn gym."

"He's probably an attorney or something, too."

"Yeah," Vanessa nodded. "That would make sense. If she's some big-shot attorney, I doubt she'd be married to a criminal. Whatever he does, I'm sure he makes good money doing it. With their combined income, it's no wonder how he can afford everything."

"They're probably on some tropical vacation together right now."

Doug's words hit her like a blow to the gut, and she started sobbing again, realizing he was probably right. Earlier that day, Mark had called her and told her that he loved her. He was probably in a luxury resort somewhere with his gorgeous wife, telling her the exact same thing. That stung. She fell back into Doug's arms, the hurt turning into resentment.

"I'm so done with him. I should have trusted my instincts. I should have demanded the truth sooner. He was so handsome and charming that I ignored every warning sign. I'm totally that girl. That dumb girl who let herself get conned by a guy with looks and a little charisma."

"I hate to say I told you so, but…"

"I'm so embarrassed."

"No more muscle heads for you, okay?" Doug told her as he massaged her shoulders. He chuckled as he added, "You need yourself a plump man who'll treat you right."

"I don't need any man. This was it. I'm done even trying."

"Just give it time."

As the extent of Mark's cheating sunk in, Vanessa's anger reared its head. She wanted to call Mark. To give him a piece of her mind for lying to her. For stringing her along. She grabbed her phone and growled, "I'm going to tell that scumbag where to go."

"No, don't." Doug stopped her by snatching her phone from her hand.

"Give me that back," she snapped, trying to pry the phone away from him.

"Listen to me, Nessa. Just listen to me," he pleaded. He looked surprised when she stopped and allowed him to continue. "You need to cut all ties with him. I know it's going to be hard. No calls. No texts. Ignore him. If he shows up at your house, refuse to answer the door. If he stops by the call center, we'll have security throw him out."

"You've seen our security, right?" Vanessa snorted. "I'm pretty sure he could wipe the floor with them."

"We'll cross that bridge when the time comes. For now, just trust me on this. If you had listened to me in the first place, you wouldn't be in this situation right now."

She had to admit that he had a point. "You got me there, but I can't just ignore him. I mean, I might be able to for a few days, but at some point, I'm going to have to call him out on this. He can't get away with it. I'm sure I'm not the first woman he's tricked, and I probably won't be the last."

"He's probably some sicko who gets off on this. Don't even give him the satisfaction. Trust me on this. Cut ties completely."

She knew herself well enough to know she wouldn't be able to cut him out completely. Not yet. Not until she'd confronted him about it. She placated Doug by telling him, "You're right. I'll just drop the whole thing."

"Good girl," he smiled.

"Thank you for being here for me."

"You never have to thank me, girl."

He hugged her again, consoling her until she'd calmed down enough to drive home. She was readying for bed when Mark finally texted her back.

*At this training thing. Get some sleep, and I'll message you tomorrow. Love you.*

She scoffed and tossed her phone aside.

"Nice try, asshole," she said as she crawled into bed.

# Chapter Ten

## *Mark*

"We have a problem," Linda announced as she frantically burst into Mark's office.

"This isn't going to be good," he murmured, noting her look of concern.

"No, no, it's not. There's been an incident in Denver."

He leaned back in his chair and let out a long groan. "Explain."

"One of our treadmills broke while a member was using it. The belt snapped, and he fell pretty hard. He's in the hospital."

"Shit." Mark rested his elbows on his desk and covered his face with his hands. "Go on," he said, his voice muffled.

"He's in rough shape but should be okay. He's understandably pissed, though. Already talking lawsuit and has been all over social media bad-mouthing the gym."

All members had to sign a safety waiver, but a defective treadmill causing serious bodily harm certainly wasn't included in it. He knew his insurance company would help with any litigation, but the negative publicity wasn't going to be good for business.

"Time to do some serious damage control," he replied, straightening his tie. "Get me on a flight to Denver right away. I want to inspect that treadmill. I need to see if it's been tampered with or anything."

"Think it could be a setup?"

"I doubt it, but you never know. We live in such a sue-happy society, it's definitely a possibility. I'll have to see for myself. I'll take a look at the treadmill, review the security footage, and talk to the guy who got hurt."

"Good. Hopefully, we can get this taken care of before it really explodes."

"This couldn't have happened at a worse time," he growled and lightly punched the arm of his chair in frustration. "Vanessa was supposed to come over tonight. I was finally going to show her my place and tell her the truth about everything. It's long overdue. The poor girl's been thinking I'm a drug dealer or gangster or something."

"Well, it'll have to wait until you get back. This should only take a couple of days."

"I know, but she's going to think I'm just making an excuse not to show her my place. She's suspicious enough already." He glanced at the time and continued, "I don't have time to tell her everything now. I need to be on a plane to Denver already. If I don't get this handled immediately, the backlash could cost a fortune. You know how word travels these days, especially through social media. This won't just hurt the Denver location. It'll echo nationwide."

"Oh, you don't have to tell me," Linda fired back. "I know how it works, so let me go book you that ticket."

"Thanks, Linda. I'm running home to pack a few things. Get me on the first available flight there. I don't care how expensive it is. Text me the details when you have them. Oh, and call Denver. Let them know I'll be there first thing tomorrow morning."

He followed her out of his office and hurried to his car. Before hitting the road, he shot Zane a quick message letting him know he had a business emergency and had to run out of town. He apologized for missing yet another workout and assured his friend that he'd be back in the gym with him as soon as possible. He took a deep breath, steeling himself for his next move. It pained him to do it, but he had to lie to Vanessa yet again since trying to cram the truth into a short phone call wasn't the route he wanted to go. He needed to talk to her in person after showing her his place, just as he'd promised. Knowing she was still at work, he called and left her a voicemail message.

"Vanessa, hey, listen, I hate to do this, but I'm going to have to push our date back. I totally spaced on this training seminar I was supposed to attend. I know, I know… I suck. Anyhow, I hope you can forgive me and promise you I'm not purposely stalling or anything. I am going to show you my place, and I am going to tell you the truth. Let me just get this training out of the way. Call or text me when you can, babe. I love you."

He felt awful before he'd even hung up. Stealing another look at the time, he debated stopping by her call center to tell her what was really going on. He couldn't imagine a woman being too upset by the revelation that her boyfriend was secretly worth close to a billion dollars, yet Vanessa was different. She was unlike any woman he'd ever met. He wasn't sure how she'd take it but knew her reaction was something he'd want to see in person.

Darting into his townhouse, he stuffed a small array of neatly folded clothes into a suitcase while giving his sister a quick rundown of what had happened. She hadn't patched things up with her husband, which came as no surprise to him. She was a very strong, very independent woman who wasn't going just to forgive and forget. She'd already filed for divorce, and he'd assured her she could continue staying with him as long as she wanted.

After hugging her and the boys' goodbye, he headed toward Brooklyn, thinking he might have enough time to talk to Vanessa face-to-face. Those plans were dashed, however, when Linda's message with the flight information came through. His flight was leaving in an hour out of LaGuardia, and given the time of day, there was no way he'd be able to make it down to Brooklyn and back up through Queens with the traffic. He'd have to shelve the conversation and hope she was still willing to have it when he got back.

He made it to LaGuardia in time and was in the middle of boarding his flight when Vanessa called. He hoped she wouldn't hear the background noise and ask why he was in an airport. Thankfully, she didn't, and although she sounded disappointed about their date being postponed, she seemed understanding and wished him luck with his training. It would give her a chance to catch up with Doug, she told him, since he'd been guilting her hard. He was relieved when she didn't ask where the training was taking place, as it was one less lie he had to tell her. They were piling up enough as it was, and that made him nervous. She might not be as forgiving as he liked to think she would be.

By the time he arrived in Denver, he was exhausted and ready for bed. Vanessa had texted him at some point during his flight, and he'd received it when he'd landed. She'd thrown in a subtle jab about his whereabouts, and unsure how to reply, he shoved his phone back in his pocket while deliberating on a response. He picked up the rental car Linda had arranged for him and made the short drive to the hotel she'd also booked. The woman was a saint. After checking into his room, he threw his suitcase on the bed and sat down next to it to send her a quick update.

*Made it! Safely in my room. You're the best, Linda.*

A moment later, a reply:

*Good! So glad you got there okay. I'll take care of everything on this end. Call or text if you need me. Get some sleep!*

He smiled at her words and scrolled to the message from Vanessa that he hadn't yet answered. He decided on the following:

*At this training thing. Get some sleep, and I'll message you tomorrow. Love you.*

As he waited for her reply, he brushed his teeth, stripped down to his boxer briefs, and climbed into bed. He turned on the television and mindlessly flipped through the channels as he continued to wait for Vanessa's reply, but when twenty minutes passed, and she still hadn't responded, he assumed she'd gone to bed and followed suit. He put his phone on silent and was out within minutes, sleeping straight through the night.

When morning came, Mark didn't waste any time. He sprang out of bed, took a quick shower, and slipped into one of the suits he'd brought. Always big on appearance, he ran a comb through his hair and adjusted his tie before grabbing a bite to eat from the hotel's continental breakfast. It wasn't enough to fill him up, but it was enough to keep him going. He shoved a sausage in his mouth and was out the door, arriving at the Denver *Buff n' Stuff* gym minutes later. He introduced himself to the staff who'd been expecting his arrival, and they looked at him like he was a celebrity. With wide eyes and smiles, they gathered around him, eagerly shaking his hand and showering him with compliments. They got a kick out of him ordering a protein shake from the gym's aptly named *Protein Bar*, a feature in every *Buff n' Stuff* location. It was a long counter lined with a variety of different protein powders and additional supplements you could have made into a shake for a few extra bucks. The *Protein Bar* was a great way for him to upsell the products provided by a manufacturer he'd signed an exclusive deal with, and thanks to promotional help from his buddy Zane's marketing firm, the idea accounted for a decent amount of the chain's annual profit.

The Denver branch manager, Debra Foley, was a pleasant woman who guided him to the broken treadmill that had been cordoned off with rope. Its belt lay torn on the running deck, and a handwritten "out of service" sign had been taped to the machine's control panel. Mark shook his head in disappointment at the sight of it.

"Who's responsible for this?" he asked.

"I… I don't get what you mean," Debra replied, looking confused as her eyes shifted from Mark to the broken treadmill and back to Mark again.

"I mean, who is responsible for this?" he asked again, gesturing to the rope and sign. "This looks terrible. Come on, now. Do you really think this is good for business? We can't have members seeing this. This thing should have been moved to the back room the second this happened."

Realizing her mistake, Debra swallowed nervously and replied, "I'm sorry, Mr. Masterson. We'll get it moved right away."

"Amateur hour," Mark muttered under his breath, shaking his head again. The sight of the busted treadmill lazily sectioned off with rope and a handwritten sign was a great way to scare away members. He hoped nobody had snapped a photo of it yet. The last thing he needed was a picture of this going around the internet.

Never afraid of a little hard work, Mark took off his suit jacket and handed it to Debra, rolled up his sleeves, and helped a couple of the staff members move the heavy treadmill into the back room. Once they had it safely out of sight from members, Mark kneeled to investigate the torn belt as Debra looked over his shoulder.

"What are you looking for?" she asked quietly.

He answered her as he continued looking over the machine. "This is a Precor, Debra. They make high-end stuff. Quality stuff. This one treadmill cost over twelve thousand dollars."

"Jesus," she gasped. "Expensive."

"Very. I know there's a first time for everything, but I've never heard of a Precor treadmill belt breaking like this. These things are built to last."

"They better be for that price."

"Exactly. I've heard of belts tearing on cheap treadmills, but never one of these." He leaned in closer and examined the torn belt again. "I can't prove it, but this belt looks like it was cut."

Debra's eyes widened in disbelief. "You think the guy did this on purpose?"

"Looks that way," Mark sighed. "I'm going to have to check out the security footage. Can you call that up for me?"

"Absolutely. Follow me."

She led him to the row of eight monitors lining the back of her office wall and pulled up a seat for him. He was no stranger to the surveillance system and was easily able to find the footage from the previous afternoon when the incident had taken place. Debra studied the monitors alongside him, all of them replaying footage of the gym from various angles. He watched the accident happen on the second monitor, and then rewound it to go over it with Debra.

"There he is," Mark said, pointing at the man as he rounded the corner into the gym's cardio area. "See how he stops to tie his shoe before he gets on the machine?"

"Mmmhmm," Debra replied, eyes narrowed as she examined the video.

"Look closely. It looks like he's pulling something out of his shoe."

"It does," she agreed, nodding.

Mark turned his attention to the third monitor, where they watched the events unfold from a much more revealing angle. Here, they could see the man quickly run what appeared to be a razor across the belt and stuff it back in his shoe. He did it fast, checking to make sure nobody was looking before making a thin cut. He knew the belt wouldn't hold up once he started jogging, and he'd been right. They continued watching as he pretended to stretch, waiting for somebody else to enter the cardio area so there would be a witness to his fall. If it hadn't been for the security cameras, which he likely hadn't even seen, as they were fairly discrete, his plan may have actually worked.

"Sneaky little bastard," Mark commented. He made a copy of the footage, and then pulled his cell phone from his jacket to record the deception with it. Vanessa had called him sometime after he'd fallen asleep, but his phone had been muted. He'd woken in business mode, so focused on getting this situation handled that he hadn't noticed the missed call until now. His phone informed him of a new voicemail message that he presumed to be from her, and as much as he wanted to listen to it, he set it aside to finish the task at hand. He'd grown used to her leaving him sweet messages and smiled at the thought of what she may have left him this time. Hearing her voice would be his reward for successfully cleaning up this mess. If all went well, it would be over soon.

"His name's Brandon Murray. He's only been a member for two weeks," Debra informed him.

"Write down his information for me if you'd be so kind. I'm going to pay him a visit."

He held his phone to the monitor and recorded the staged accident. Taking the details Debra had jotted down for him and putting his suit jacket back on, he thanked her for her time and made his way to the hospital to meet with Mr. Murray, a young man in his early twenties who, in Mark's opinion, had a very punch able face. He looked like an arrogant, self-entitled brat who'd never put in a hard day of work in his life. One of his legs was in a cast, and his left wrist was wrapped in a bandage.

"About time you got here," he snorted. "You always keep your clients waiting this long?"

Mark pulled a chair over to Brandon's bed and sat down, steepling his fingers and cracking a knowing grin. "Do you know who I am?"

"You're my lawyer, right? My mom told me you were coming." He looked Mark over and continued, "I guess you had to go pump some iron first. Really professional. I'm laying here in pain, and you're off lifting weights."

Mark's grin widened, and he replied slowly, "Oh, I'm not your lawyer."

"Then who are you?"

"I'm Mark Masterson."

"Am I supposed to know that name?" Brandon scoffed.

"You know the gym you tried to defraud? I own it. I own them all."

Brandon Murray shifted nervously in his bed. "I don't know what you're talking about."

"I think you do," Mark replied, casually pulling his cell phone from his pocket.

"Your defective treadmill broke my leg and shattered my goddamn wrist. We don't have to take it to court. I'm willing to settle right now for five million dollars."

"I have a better deal in mind. You're going to hop online and apologize for trying to scam me. You're going to admit that you cut that belt and that you're a sack of shit."

"You can't prove that," Brandon countered.

"That you're a sack of shit?" Mark laughed. "I can, actually. By posting this video of you slicing the belt with that little razor blade you were hiding in your shoe."

He held up his phone and played the video he'd recorded of the surveillance footage. When he replayed it, Brandon refused to watch. Rather, he stared blankly at the wall with his jaw clenched for a moment before finally muttering softly, "Fine. You got me."

"Not so smart now, are you?" Mark smirked, stuffing his phone back into his pocket. "Didn't even notice the cameras. Brilliant."

"I said fine!" Brandon hissed. "Now, leave me alone."

"I want that apology first."

"Okay, I'm sorry, alright? Now just… just get out of here."

Mark groaned and rubbed his temples. "I meant online, moron. Take that little phone of yours," he motioned to Brandon's cell phone lying on the bedside table, "and post that public apology. I'll wait."

Brandon hesitated but did as told. "There. Done. Now go."

"Show me," Mark insisted.

"So demanding, God," Brandon muttered, handing over his phone.

Mark read his update and nodded his approval. "That'll do."

"Good, now you can leave."

"Trust me; I'm in no mood to stay." Mark stood to leave and added, "Just know this. If you delete that post you made, I'll be sharing this video and pressing charges. You're lucky I'm not doing both anyway. Step foot in one of my gyms again, and I'll make sure you go away for a long time."

*"Go!"* Brandon yelled, pointing at the door with his good hand.

Mark left the room with a satisfied smirk and called Linda to update her. She was thrilled to hear the good news and booked him a flight home as he recounted what had transpired. With that call out of the way, he excitedly dialed his voicemail to treat himself to Vanessa's voice finally. He froze in his tracks, his heart racing as he listened to the message she'd left him.

"Hello, Mark Mitchell. Or should I call you by your real name, Mark Masterson? Oops! Looks like somebody found out the truth. I just wanted to say a quick 'fuck you' for lying to me. If you were trying to make me feel stupid, you did a really good job. I not-so-kindly invite you to never talk to me again. I was dumb enough to fall for your lies once, but I won't fall for them twice. In fact, why don't you—"

Her message abruptly ended in what sounded like a thud and a faint scuffle. He wasn't sure what that was all about, but he was sure that she was pissed. Very pissed. Her words had crushed his good mood, leaving him with a knot in his stomach and a lump in his throat. His mind raced, wondering how she could have found out and why her reaction had been so hateful. He always assumed she'd be a little upset if she learned the truth before he got a chance to tell her, but to be this mad? In the grand scheme of things, his lies hadn't been that awful. He'd lied about his last name and being the owner of a hugely successful chain of gyms. He was fairly certain most women would at least allow an explanation they'd likely find excusable. His net worth was reason alone for most women to forgive a little white lie about his last name. But then, Vanessa wasn't like most women. She'd told him about her trust issues, yet he'd kept lying to her. On one hand, her deep, visceral response didn't make sense. On the other, it made all the sense in the world.

He needed to get back to New York to talk to her.

# Chapter Eleven
## *Vanessa*

Tossing and turning in bed, Vanessa couldn't stop replaying the video in her mind. Mark kisses his wife. Telling her he loved her. She returned the words. He hugged his two kids. The more she thought about it, the angrier she got. She'd turned her phone off and stuffed it between her mattress and box spring, hoping it would deter her from calling him. Bolting out of bed, she pulled her phone from its hiding place and held it in her hand as she paced her living room, deciding whether or not she should call him. Doug had advised her against it, but he had no idea what it was like to feel this hurt. This betrayed. She was as mad at herself as she was at him for setting herself up for this. She knew something was off that he wasn't being completely truthful with her, but she never thought he was hiding a wife and kids.

Wherever he was, she figured he'd be asleep and wasn't surprised when his phone went to voicemail. She was in the middle of leaving him a message when it happened.

"I was dumb enough to fall for your lies once, but I won't fall for them twice. In fact, why don't you—"

That sentence would have ended with "tell your wife and kids I say hi" had she not fallen to the floor, her body convulsing in pain from the wave of electricity coursing through her. Her phone flew from her hand as her muscles cramped and her body spasmed. Having never been tased before, it took her a moment to realize that's what had happened. Standing over her was somebody dressed in black, their face concealed with a frightening goat mask. From their clothing and build—slumped shoulders with a pronounced belly— she could tell they were male and had a fairly good idea who it was. She tried to scream for help but could barely get the words out. With no ability to fight back, she lay defenseless, wearing only her bra and panties as the masked intruder stepped on her phone, crushing it under a heavy black boot. When she managed to inch away from them, the assailant hit her with the taser a second time, completely immobilizing her. The pain was unlike anything she'd ever felt, and although she'd lost all motor skills, she was still aware of her surroundings. She watched in terror as her attacker pulled a bottle from his pocket and emptied its contents onto a rag before pressing it to her face with a gloved hand. He sat on her chest, pinning her arms down with his knees while he continued to hold the rag over her mouth and nose. She knew she was being chloroformed, but unlike what she'd seen in movies and on television, it took much longer than expected for its effects to hit her. After a minute, she began to regain control of her body but was still too weakened to defend herself. She clawed at the man's hands, trying to pry them from her face, but it proved futile. Moments later, the room faded to black as she lost consciousness.

Vanessa awoke in a fog, her mind muddled from the chloroform. When she moved, whatever cushioned surface she was laying on creaked beneath her. As her senses returned, she realized she'd been placed on a small cot in what appeared to be a basement, a chain wrapped around her robed waist that had been securely fastened to a load-bearing support beam. She groaned and sat up, her head still throbbing from the drug that had knocked her out. Pressing her palms into her closed eyes, she massaged her temples with her thumbs, trying to shake the remaining cloudiness. The panic began to set in as the remnants of the compound left her system.

She struggled to recall what had happened, but the memories only came in small flashes. Had she been raped? She didn't feel like she had, but couldn't be sure. Disconcerting was the black bathrobe she was now wearing that she didn't recognize as one of hers.

With a lump of dread in her throat, she opened the robe, hoping to see the matching bra and panties she'd remembered going to bed in. Her chest heaved, and she began to sob at the realization she'd been stripped of them. The overwhelming sense of violation was too much for her. She lost it, rivulets of tears running down her face as she envisioned the awful things he could have done to her while she was unconscious.

She calmed herself enough to take in her surroundings and dried her eyes with the robe. A study of the room told her it was definitely a basement. It had that familiar musty smell and dank feel, and the support beam she was secured to meant there was an upper level. Concrete walls and a small, boarded-over window near the ceiling were further evidence that she was at least partially underground. The floor, also concrete, looked like it had recently been swept clean, possibly in preparation for her arrival. A jug of water sat beside her bed, along with a few magazines and a handful of granola bars. At the foot of her bed was a five-gallon bucket with a roll of toilet paper and hand sanitizer next to it. She hoped that didn't mean what she thought it did.

A small door across the room likely led upstairs, and she knew it was probably locked. The basement was dimly illuminated by a low-watt light bulb that hung from the ceiling, its switch on the other side of the room beyond her reach. Aside from the items that seemed to have been left out purposely for her, the space was rather bare. Using both hands, she pulled on the chain, realizing quickly that it wasn't going to budge. One end had been looped around her waist and padlocked; the other looped around the support beam and also padlocked. Still reeling from the sedation, she stumbled as she attempted to stand but managed to get to her feet. The chain rattled as she picked it up and pulled on it again, to no avail. She gave it one more shot, summoning all the strength she had before giving up and letting it drop to the floor.

"Fuck!" she muttered angrily. Her heart began to race as the severity of her situation hit her, gripping her with fear. Frantic, she tugged at the chain around her waist, hoping she could pull it down around her. Unable to work it past her hips, she tried pulling it up, but that proved futile as well. Shaking, she sat down on the cot, rocking back and forth while holding herself. There was no doubt in her mind who was responsible for this.

Seconds later, the doorknob sounded, and she heard the distinct click of it unlocking. The door creaked open, and her abductor, still dressed in black and wearing the disturbing goat mask, entered the room carrying a metal folding chair. He set it down at a distance she was sure he'd predetermined she couldn't reach, given the length of the chain. Safely out of her range, he unfolded it and took a seat. As she sat trembling, her masked captor started at her, saying nothing. The cold, black eyes of the goat mask bore a hole through her, the room eerily quiet.

"H-Harold," she stuttered, breaking the maddening silence. "You need to let me go."

There was no response. He continued to stare at her, hands resting on his lap as he watched her through the lifeless expression of the mask. She sensed he was enjoying every second of her panic, reveling in the fear he'd struck into her.

"Please. You don't need to do this," Vanessa pleaded. Starting at the goat mask was like staring at the face of the devil himself. "You can just let me go, and we'll forget all about this, okay? Just... just unlock this chain, and we'll pretend this never happened. I won't go to the authorities, I promise."

Again, nothing but that same dead stare. She swallowed hard, nerves on edge as he simply sat there, looking at her in silence.

*"Fucking let me go!"* she screamed, springing off the cot and across the room. The chain grew taut inches before she reached him, snapping her back at a speed that knocked her off of her feet. She fell hard, landing on her ass and groaning in pain. The whiplash had hurt her neck more than anything. Wincing, she tried to rub the kink out when her abductor finally made a sound. He began to laugh, but it sounded like it had been modified electronically.

"Are... are you seriously laughing at me?" she hissed, looking at him with hatred.

"I was waiting for that," he replied.

She was right. He'd modified his voice using a digital voice changer. He'd placed the microphone inside the mask, its cord running down his side to a small speaker attached to his belt loop. She could tell it was a cheap device thanks to the words "Voice Disguiser" printed on the side in a childish font. Since Halloween was right around the corner, he'd likely picked it up at some local Halloween store. As crappy as it was, it worked well enough to conceal his real voice.

"Really?" she asked sarcastically, pointing to the speaker. "I know it's you, Harold. You can cut the theatrics."

"You should have given me a chance," he replied, ignoring her remark and continuing to use the voice changer. "We could have been so good together."

"No, we couldn't have because I'm sane, and you're a complete lunatic," she fired back bitterly. She realized her mistake the second she'd made it. If she wanted to make it out of this basement alive, she needed to convince Harold that they had a chance. She corrected herself and ran a hand through her hair seductively. "I mean, a little crazy is a good thing. Maybe we can start again? Give us a shot?"

"Nice try," he said flatly. "Wow, you really do think I'm stupid."

She'd changed direction too fast and chastised herself for not being subtle enough. She tried again, kneeling in front of him and looking up at him innocently. "No, I really don't. I mean it, we could really have something if we just—"

"Enough!" he snapped loudly enough to make the small speaker crackle. He lowered his voice and continued, "You may be a lot of things, but a good actress isn't one of them. Drop the routine."

"What do you want from me?" she asked, her brow lowered in anger again.

He stared at her a moment. She wished she could see his face instead of the expressionless goat mask. He finally answered, "For you to want me."

"Harold… you attacked me. You drugged me. Stripped me naked. Did Lord knows what with me, then chained me up in this basement?" She shook her head while looking at him in disgust. "Do you really think I could ever want you after what you've done?"

He leaned in so close she could smell the rubber mask. "Yes."

"Then you really are crazy."

"Have you ever heard of Stockholm syndrome?"

"Oh, Jesus," she scoffed, rolling her eyes. "You really think you can keep me down here until I fall in love with you?"

"It might take a month. It might take a year. Hell, it might take ten years. But eventually? Yes. You will love me. When I'm the only thing you know, the only thing you have… you will love me."

"You… you can't keep me down here that long. Somebody will find me."

"You think anybody's going to find you down here?" he laughed.

It pained her to think he could be right. After the voicemail message she'd left Mark, he certainly wouldn't be looking for her. Doug would notice her missing, and she liked to think he'd contact the authorities, but they'd be hard-pressed to find any leads if he didn't think to mention Harold. If anything, they'd likely suspect Mark, assuming he'd murdered her to hide the affair from his wife and kids. She could only hope Doug would pass Harold's name along to the police. The maniac had crushed her phone, and there was no telling what he'd done with the remains, but the cops might be able to get his number from her phone records. She'd deleted her account on the dating site, wiping away any trace of communication that might have been left between them there. Phone records would be the only way.

All these thoughts ran through her mind as Harold sat watching her through the painted black eyes of the goat mask. "You know I'm right."

"They'll trace it back to you. Somehow. A phone call. A text message. They'll come looking for me here. Just let me go now, and you won't get in any trouble."

"Not likely," he chuckled. "You should have just given me a chance. Instead, you fell for that 'roided-up playboy. You knew he was a liar but ignored it because he was good-looking. I never expected you to be such a shallow bitch."

"That's not true," she began to counter but wasn't able to finish. Her poor choices had made it hard for her to defend herself, and Harold's words weren't too far off the mark. She did know he was lying, but it wasn't just his looks and charm that had kept her quiet. It was how well he had treated her. How deeply she'd already fallen in love with him. She'd never considered herself to be a shallow person, but she had to admit his gorgeous face and remarkable physique had played a role in the attraction, at least initially. Of course, she couldn't tell Harold that.

"Oh, it's true. And look at where it got you," her captor taunted. "He broke your heart. I would have never done that, Vanessa. I would have never lied to you."

With no argument for that, she steered the conversation back to where it had been. "This doesn't have to go any further. Just let me go, and you can walk away from this. If you keep me, they will find me, and you'll be going away for a very long time."

"I don't care," he shrugged. "Nothing matters if I can't have you."

"Harold…"

"Did you know," he said, leaning forward in his chair again, "that I've been in love with you since the moment we met? You're all I think about."

"We had one date," she reminded him. "One date that ended… well, you remember."

He reverted back to saying nothing, only staring at her through the goat mask. The silence was long and uncomfortable.

"You don't even know me!" she finally burst.

"I know you better than you think." She couldn't see his face but sensed he was smiling. Standing to leave, he collected his metal chair and folded it back up, tucking it under his arm. "I'll be back later. You need time to miss me."

"Harold," she called after him as he was leaving. He stopped and looked at her over his shoulder. She swallowed nervously and asked, "When I was passed out… did you…"

"No," he replied. "When I finally have you, it will be because you want me."

With that, he left, locking the door behind him.

# Chapter Twelve
## *Mark*

"I don't know, man," Mark grunted as he pushed out his last rep and re-racked the weight bar. "She sounded pissed."

"I don't care who they are. No woman would be upset to find out her boyfriend is rich," Zane replied.

A week had gone by with no word from Vanessa. She'd warned him not to contact her again, but there was no way Mark could let her walk out of his life like that. He'd left her several voicemails and text messages, careful not to overdo it so he didn't come across as another Harold, yet they'd all gone unanswered.

"You didn't hear the voicemail message," Mark told him, shaking his head.

Mark had fallen hard for Vanessa, and her unexpectedly abrupt end to their relationship had hurt in a way he'd never felt before. For the first time in his life, he'd been on the receiving end of a breakup, leaving him with a broken heart. It was a pain he'd never experienced until now, and it made even the simplest of tasks difficult. He couldn't take his mind off of what had happened, making it nearly impossible to focus on his routine. Unable to concentrate yet again, he pushed through his workout without the intensity he usually put in. Zane had noticed his lack of effort but was understanding, listening to his friend instead of ribbing him. Mark was appreciative of that, and after their obligatory fist bump, this one as half-hearted as they'd been all week, he drove back home to his townhouse, which now felt lonely and cold.

He kept his phone on him at all times, desperately hoping she would reply. Checking for the hundredth time to make sure its ringer was on, he set it on his counter as he made dinner, glancing at it every few minutes in hopes it would sound. When the day ended with still no response, he crawled into bed, knowing he had another sleepless night to look forward to. He was right and headed into work the following morning, looking noticeably tired.

"You look like shit," Linda greeted as he trudged her toward his office. She followed him in and looked at him with concern. "Mark, you need to go home. Take the day off. Rest."

"Pointless," Mark sighed. "Can't sleep. I've been trying, believe me."

"Then go see her."

Linda had been repeating this all week, insisting that he must go speak to Vanessa. If she had heard how angry Vanessa had sounded in that voicemail, however, she might not be pushing the idea on him. He still couldn't believe the outrage in the girl's voice. How fired up she'd been over what he thought was a rather petty offense.

"I want to, but she's obviously still upset since she hasn't called or messaged me back."

"She's a woman. We're stubborn. Trust me, I know. Like I've been saying, she's probably waiting for you to go talk to her face-to-face."

"None of this would have happened if I'd been honest with her from the beginning," he huffed. "If you hadn't made me lie to her, we'd be—"

"Excuse me?" Linda scoffed, cutting him off mid-sentence. "Don't try to pin this on me. I only wanted you to hide your name and money from her for the first date to make sure she wasn't a gold digger like the rest of them. I never told you to keep lying to her. You were supposed to tell her the truth ages ago."

She turned on her heel and stormed out of the room. Sleep-deprived and frustrated, he groaned and rubbed his eyes, silently scolding himself for the mess he'd gotten himself into. He knew what he had to do. He took a moment to compose himself before heading out of his office.

"I'm sorry," he said earnestly, stopping at Linda's desk. "About what I said in there. This is my fault, not yours. Please, forgive me."

"I forgave you the minute you said it," she smiled up at him. "Now go find her, handsome boy."

"Thank you, Linda."

He hoped Vanessa would be as forgiving but knew it was a long shot. If she'd been willing to hear him out, she would have returned one of his messages by now. Perhaps Linda was right, and she was simply waiting for him to seek her out. He wasn't sure what to think anymore but knew he couldn't go another day without talking to her.

It was still early, only a little after 9:00 am, but Vanessa had been working morning shifts so they could spend their afternoons together. He'd been ducking out early so they could see each other before his evening workout, and the schedule had been working well for them until her explosion. If she hadn't changed her shifts around, he knew the best place to find her would be the call center. He tried to stay positive as he headed into Brooklyn to see her and hopefully smooth things over.

He'd stopped by the call center a few times over the course of their romance, so he knew his way around the place well enough. The first occasion had been to surprise her with flowers. The second and third had been to spend her lunch break with her. It was a bit of a drive, but it was always worth it. Taking the elevator to the building's second floor, he made his way past the sea of cubicles, dividing one client support specialist from the next. The room was a low murmur of voices as employees did their best to placate their callers.

Doug saw him and bolted from his cubicle, intercepting him before he could reach Vanessa's office.

"She doesn't want to see you."

"I get that, but I need to talk to her," Mark said, stepping by him and continuing toward her office.

Doug jumped in front of him and stopped him again. "I told you she doesn't want to see you, so just leave before I have you thrown out."

"Oh, I'd love to see that happen," Mark chuckled. "Now stand aside."

"Look, she's not even here, okay?" Doug sighed, realizing his threat wasn't going to work. "She hasn't been in all week."

Mark flashed him a look of disbelief. "Sure, she hasn't."

"Go see for yourself." Doug motioned to her office, and Mark stuck his head in, noting her empty desk. He didn't think she'd be immature enough to hide behind it, but he had to check to make sure. She wasn't there, of course, and he shook his head at the idiocy of the idea. Lack of sleep and exasperation were catching up to him.

"Happy?" Doug asked sarcastically.

"Not really, no. Listen, if you talk to her, tell her I'm looking for her. Tell her—"

"Yeah, I won't be doing that. She's done with you and your lies. You messed her up so bad she's missed a week of work I know she can't afford. The last thing she needs is to hear from you."

Mark felt his frustration turning to anger but tried not to lose his cool with the chubby little man. "Have you heard from her at all?"

"No. She's been ignoring everybody. She's probably locked herself in her house trying to get over you." He saw Mark's contemplative look and knew what he was thinking. "Do *not* go over there. Just leave her alone. You've done enough damage."

He didn't bother replying since their conversation had reached a dead end. Doug's words weren't going to deter him, not with Vanessa's home so close. With her work ethic rivaling his, something about her missing an entire week didn't sit right with him. He was beginning to think she might be in trouble. His deceit had clearly upset her, that much he knew from the voicemail message that had been seared into his mind, but he couldn't imagine her missing a full week of work over it. Even with her reduced mortgage—that she still didn't know he'd been responsible for—Doug was right: she couldn't afford to miss that many hours.

Minutes later, he pulled up to her house, noticing right away that her car was parked in the driveway. He hurried up her front steps and collected himself before knocking. When she didn't answer, his knocks grew louder.

"Vanessa? I know you're in there. We need to talk. I can explain everything, I swear."

He listened for footsteps or any sound coming from inside her house. Nothing. He knocked again, this time even louder.

"Vanessa? Are you okay? Please, just say something."

Again, only silence. He glanced back at her car in the driveway, a sinking feeling in his stomach. If she were asleep, his incessant knocking definitely would have woken her by now. If she were simply ignoring him, she probably would have snapped and chased him off of her property already. He lingered, hoping he'd at least see her peek through a curtain. He needed a sign—something, anything—to let him know she was okay. If she flung the door open to tell him off, perhaps threatening to call the cops, he'd take it just to know she was alive and well.

He waited another ten minutes, pounding on the door and yelling her name in between pacing her small porch. As a last resort, he tried letting himself in, but the door was locked. He was tempted to try a window but didn't want to get arrested for breaking and entering. It was broad daylight, and he'd already attracted the attention of several neighbors. Giving up, he rooted through his glove box for a piece of paper and a pen. He jotted down a quick note and wedged it in her door, praying she'd find it.

*Vanessa,*

*I'm worried sick. Please let me know if you're okay.*

*I love you.*

*Mark*

# Chapter Thirteen
## *Vanessa*

A month had gone by. At least, Vanessa was fairly certain it had been a month. The basement's only window had been boarded over, but enough light crept through the cracks to let her know when it was day and when it was night. Harold's routine had also helped her keep track of the days. She could hear the floorboards above her creak when he woke in the morning and hear them again when he arrived home from wherever it was he went all day. With each passing day, she ripped a small tear up the bottom of one of the magazine pages by her bed. With nothing to write with, this was her only option, and it worked well enough.

It had been a long, torturous month. She still couldn't believe that nobody had come for her. She'd spent the first week screaming until she lost her voice, hoping somebody passing by the house would hear her cries and send the authorities. She'd quickly learned Harold's schedule and would wait until he left, presumably for work, before yelling her voice raw. She'd given up on that plan, instead focusing on a way to escape. With no usable tools, however, freeing herself of the chain seemed impossible. She'd managed to pry a small spring from the cot and had shaped it into a makeshift lock pick, working on the padlock on her waist throughout the day. When she failed to make any progress, she eventually gave up. There was nothing she could fashion into a weapon, and even if she'd found something, Harold rarely got close enough for her to use it. Her assault and subsequent abduction had been carefully planned, that much was apparent, leaving little hope of rescue or escape. Her only option was to wait it out. To memorize every move he made and look for vulnerabilities in him rather than her surroundings.

She'd recalled him telling her on their first and only date that he'd been living with his mother. Since the house was silent while he was gone, she assumed this must be the new place he'd been talking about getting. Every so often, she'd hear the faint sound of a cat meowing, but aside from that, the house was unsettlingly quiet when he wasn't home. She'd pass the time lying on the cot, staring up at the ceiling that was scattered with cobwebs. The stack of magazines he'd left her didn't serve much entertainment. By the second week, she'd read them all cover to cover four times.

Almost every day was the same. The floorboards would creak, signaling that Harold was awake. A short while later, he'd unlock the door and slide her a plate of food, always wearing the same black clothes and the goat mask that had lost its creepiness and was now bordering on silly. He wouldn't stay long and would never say anything. After a few days of this, she realized it was because he didn't bother with the voice changer in the mornings. She figured the thing must have been a pain to wire into the mask, and, with his rush to leave for work, he couldn't be bothered. She'd decided the mask and voice changer were a way for him to disassociate himself from the horrible acts he was committing.

He'd arrive home sometime in the late afternoon or early evening. She could hear his footsteps as he made his way through the house, appearing several minutes later wearing his disguise. He'd use a broom handle with a bent coat hanger taped to the end of it as a means of retrieving her breakfast plate without entering her range of attack. He used the same technique to empty the bucket serving as her toilet. He'd hook the bent hanger onto the bucket's handle and drag it across the floor to him, then bring it upstairs to empty and wash it, returning moments later to reposition it at the end of her bed. This one humiliating act, performed every day, stripped of her dignity and made her feel like little more than a caged animal.

With her bucket cleaned, he'd head back upstairs and reappear with another plate of food for her. After sliding it across the floor, he'd once again trod back up the rickety wooden stairs to have his dinner alone. She could only assume this was because he couldn't eat with his mask on. Why he continued wearing the thing was beyond her comprehension since she knew who he was. If it wasn't to distance himself from his crimes, she couldn't find any other explanation for it. Trying to understand the machinations of a madman was an exercise in futility.

She was usually done eating by the time he rejoined her with his voice changer, taking a seat in the metal folding chair he'd been leaving in the same place. He'd marked a spot on the floor under the chair's front right leg that indicated he was safely out of her reach. Before taking a seat, he'd always check to make sure the chair hadn't slid forward, putting him at risk of attack. He was meticulous; she gave him that, and his attention to detail made her nervous. If he was thorough enough to think of things as little as marking the location of his chair, it didn't bode well for her chances of rescue.

Once seated, they'd spend the next two hours having what he referred to as their "evening chat." In the beginning, he'd made her talk under fear of being tased if she didn't. He wanted her to open up to him. To tell him all of her hopes and dreams. Her fears and nightmares. He'd volunteer his wishes and fantasies, most of which included her in the role of his loving, adoring wife. At one point, the cheap voice changer he insisted on using died while he was in the middle of a sentence, and she'd almost heard his real voice. He'd caught it just in time, changing out the battery with a spare he had readied in his pocket.

It was clear to her that these evening chats were quite important to him. In his deranged mind, he actually thought she'd develop feelings for him if they spent enough time getting to know each other. She went along with it, pretending to care about his feelings while imagining blowing the goat mask off his ugly face with a shotgun. She hated the sound of his cheaply digitized voice and knew if she made it out of his basement alive, the memory of it would haunt her forever.

Before going to bed, he'd feed her once more and slide her another jug of water. He always left the light on, even at night, something she appreciated since the thought of being in pitch black terrified her. The light was dim enough not to disturb her sleep, which was good since sleeping had become her preferred method of passing time. She imagined this was how inmates in prison must feel; only they had the luxury of television to help stave off boredom.

Every few days, he'd allow her to bathe using a bucket of soapy water and a large sponge. He'd watch from his chair, demanding she disrobe and waving the taser at her if she hesitated. She'd tug the robe out from under the chain and set it on the cot as she cleaned herself, turning her back to him in an effort to conceal herself. During one of her sponge baths, she made the mistake of glancing over her shoulder and caught him with his hands down his pants, masturbating. She quickly looked away and hurried to finish so she could get herself back into the robe.

That was how her month had been spent. Thirty days exactly, if the small tears she'd been making in the magazine were correct. She counted them again and sighed, knowing it would soon be time to start again on a new page since the bottom of the first didn't have much room left. She'd spent over four weeks in Harold's captivity and was no closer to caring about him now than she was when he'd first abducted her. If anything, she hated him more.

Curled up on the small, uncomfortable cot, she found herself missing Mark and fantasizing about him rescuing her and kicking down the basement door, tearing the mask off of Harold's head and beating his face unrecognizable, breaking the chain with his incredible strength, scooping her up in his big arms and carrying her to safety. It was stupid, she knew, but she'd fallen in love with the guy, and in horror, she was now living. His lies didn't seem to matter. His transgressions paled in comparison to Harold's.

Footsteps above her snapped her out of her thoughts. Minutes later, Harold appeared for their evening chat and took his seat in the folding chair. Vanessa was in no mood to deal with him today.

"Will you just take that ridiculous mask off already?"

He folded his arms across his chest and shook his head no.

"I've already seen your face. What are you going to do, wear it forever? What's your plan, anyway? I fall in love with you, and you wear that mask for the rest of our lives?" She paused and added with a sarcastic roll of her eyes, "Because that makes sense."

He sat in silence for a moment before replying, "I'll take it off when you're ready to have me."

"Yeah, well, I hate to break it to you, but that's never going to happen."

"I don't like your attitude."

"I don't like your stupid fucking face," she spat, standing up and approaching him defiantly.

"That's no way to talk to your future husband," he said, also rising to his feet. "What's gotten into you today?"

"Oh, Jesus," she groaned, rubbing her temples. "I'm so sick of that dumb robot voice. What little kid did you steal that from, anyway?"

The small speaker on his belt loop crackled as his voice raised. "You will show me respect!"

"Or what? You'll tase me again because you're too much of a pussy to smack me around?" She'd riled him up, and it felt good. He was flustered for the first time, and she knew that left him open for a mistake.

"I'm warning you. Calm down or—"

"Or you'll do what, exactly?" she stopped him. "Cry? Are you going to cry? Cry to your mommy?" She continued to provoke him, smirking as they stared each other down. "You're so pathetic. Can't get a woman, so you have to kidnap one? What a fucking loser."

Triggered, he lunged forward and tried to hit her, but the punch—which looked more like a slap—was slow and sloppy. She easily blocked it and it and kneed him in the gut, causing him to bend over in pain. In doing so, the voice changer came loose and fell to the concrete floor. She reacted without thinking, slamming her foot down on the device and crushing it beneath her heel. He backed out of her reach before she could finish her attack and looked at the destroyed voice changer. Breathing heavily from the adrenaline surge, she eyed him worriedly, unsure how he was going to handle her insubordination. As she thought, he didn't take it well. He released a low growl and darted out of the room, returning seconds later with the taser. He moved toward her, his outstretched arm holding the weapon, but paused before reaching her, seemingly reluctant to use it. His chest heaved in anger, and she could hear his labored breathing through the mask. He was visibly angry, yet didn't shock her. In a baffling move, he slowly backed away before abruptly turning and leaving the basement, locking the door behind him.

She wasn't sure what had stopped him from sending her to the floor with a wave of crippling electricity. Perhaps he didn't want to feel like a coward by tasing her instead of using his own brute force, but it felt like more than that. It felt like he was afraid of her.

# Chapter Fourteen
## *Mark*

It had been over a month since Vanessa's disappearance, leaving little doubt that she'd been the victim of foul play. Mark had filed a missing person's report after returning to her home the day after leaving his note and finding it still wedged in her front door. Her employer and her mother had also filed a missing person's report, and with three separate reports filed, the police were taking the case quite seriously.

He'd been dragged down to Brooklyn's 66th Precinct and grilled by two detectives playing the good cop, bad cop routine. Both seemed sure that he was the reason Vanessa had gone missing.

"We know you did it, dirt bag," Detective Mueller growled, playing the bad cop role with an Oscar-worthy performance. "Just make it easier on yourself and confess now."

Detective Patterson, acting the part of a good cop, spoke much softer in an understanding tone. "Look, we know you'd been lying to her about a few things. We heard she got pretty mad at you. Called to chew you out. What happened, Mark? Did you go see her? Things get out of hand, and you lose your temper? Hit her? Maybe she didn't wake up, so you panicked and hid her body? I'm sure it was probably just an accident. Just tell us what you did with her. Where we can find her."

"I'm telling you," Mark had pleaded, "I don't know where she is. All I know is I went to Colorado, and when I got back the next day, she was gone. You're supposed to help figure out the rest."

*"We already figured it out, asshole!"* Detective Mueller yelled, bringing his fist down on the interrogation room desk. "You had yourself some 'roid rage and killed her. She broke up with you, and your precious ego couldn't take it. Now tell us where she is!"

After the relentless interrogation that lasted almost two hours, Mark stopped being cooperative and lawyered up, calling his sister to the station to represent him. They were set on pinning the disappearance on him and showed little interest in pursuing other avenues. In their mind, he was the perfect suspect for the crime. They painted him as a typical rich guy who thought he was above the law, a musclebound control freak with a violent temper. When he'd mentioned Harold, they'd jotted the name down but didn't seem to lend it any credence. With no evidence to charge him, he'd walked out knowing they weren't done with him.

"They sure have it out for me," he sighed, shaking his head.

His sister was quick to agree. "Jesus, I'll say. Somebody must have pointed a finger at you."

"I know her friend Doug isn't my biggest fan, but I don't think he'd accuse me. I'd say it was the guy who'd been harassing her, but it sounds like they haven't even talked to him yet. None of this makes any sense."

He'd hired a private investigator the same day he'd filed his missing person's report, knowing it could be another week or two before the police actively began looking for Vanessa. He wasn't going to sit back and wait while Harold did unthinkable things to the woman he loved. The cops would likely track the creep down at some point, but there was no telling how long that would take. They'd have to secure a court order for Vanessa's phone records, then find the two numbers he'd been bothering her from before finally tracing it back to him. Leaving the police station after the grueling interrogation, he thanked himself for having started the ball rolling weeks earlier. He parted ways with his sister and called his investigator, Michael McKeever.

"Michael, its Mark Masterson calling you again. Look, I know I've been a pain, but I really need an update. Tell me something good."

"I've been digging but still don't have much to go on. She didn't have much of a social circle. I've only had a few small leads, and they've turned up dry."

"What about Harold? Have you tracked him down yet? He's the only lead you should be focusing on."

"The only chance I'd even have of finding him would be through either her phone or her phone records."

"We need those phone records, Mike. Find a way to make it happen. It's been weeks now. We should have had them already."

Mark heard him release an exasperated sigh before replying, "I don't know how many times I have to tell you this. I can't get them without a subpoena, and I just don't have that kind of power."

"There has to be a way. Please… I'm begging you, here."

"I'd help you if you could. I'm good, but as good as I am, there's no getting phone records without going through a judge. Unless—"

McKeever purposely stopped himself short. Mark prodded him to finish. "Unless what?"

"Come on, man. Don't make me say it."

"Unless I grease a few palms?"

"You didn't hear that from me," McKeever was quick to clarify.

"Understood. Can you at least tell me who her carrier is?"

Mark heard papers rustle as the private investigator held him for a moment. "Looks like… Verizon." There was another pause and the sound of keystrokes before, "There are a few Verizon locations in Brooklyn. If I were you, I'd go the one nearest her house and see if you can work out a deal, if you know what I mean."

"I'm in Brooklyn right now, actually," Mark replied. "I'll take it from here. Thank you, Michael."

"Wish there were more I could do."

The location closest to her home refused to help and kicked him out after offering the clerk an envelope stuffed with money in exchange for Vanessa's phone records. He tried the same approach at the second location and also got kicked out, this time with the threat of police involvement. With no other option, he had to try again, and the third time seemed to be the charm. Only one employee was working and greeted him with a sigh as if having to deal with a customer was putting him out. He looked to be in his late teens and reminded Mark of Brandon Murray, the young man who had brazenly tried to rip him off. Right away, he knew he'd get what he needed.

"Yeah?" the kid greeted, looking thoroughly unimpressed.

"Nice attitude," Mark scoffed.

The young employee started over with a big, fake smile and an exaggerated niceness oozing with sarcasm. "Hello, sir, welcome to Verizon Wireless. Golly, it sure is a nice day out! How can I help you today?"

"Look, I'm not going to waste my time or yours. I'm going to cut right to the chase here. I'm looking for somebody. My girl's been missing for a month now. Before she disappeared, she had a stalker who was always blowing up her phone. I'm pretty sure he's the reason she's missing, but the only way I can get his name is from her phone records."

A customer entered and began browsing the store's array of phones. The kid looked at the woman with the same lack of enthusiasm he'd shown Mark moments earlier.

"Have you, like, called the cops?" he asked.

Mark lowered his voice so as not to be overheard. "Of course. They'll be getting her phone records from you guys soon, but it's not fast enough. I need to find this guy now. There might be a chance she's still alive."

Mark pulled the envelope from the pocket of his suit jacket and slid it across the counter. The kid glanced inside, and his eyes grew wide.

"Holy shit!" he blurted, drawing notice from the customer. She flashed him a disapproving look and turned her attention back to the phones she'd been browsing. In a hushed voice, the kid leaned over the counter and asked, "How much is this?"

"Five thousand dollars," Mark replied quietly, casting a look over his shoulder to make sure the woman wasn't listening in. "It's yours if you get me those phone records."

"I could lose my job…," the kid whispered.

"I won't tell if you don't," Mark winked.

The kid was smart enough to realize their hushed conversation would rouse the woman's suspicion and played along in his normal tone. After clearing his throat, he said, "Okay, sir, I'd be happy to retrieve your wife's information. What did you say her name was?"

"Vanessa Claire," Mark replied, and then slowly spelled her last name to make sure the kid got it right. "I need the records for the last two months, please."

"Ah, found her. One moment, sir."

Within a minute, he had the phone records in his hand. He thanked the young employee and tapped on the envelope, giving him the signal to take it. The kid discreetly slid it off of the counter and into the back pocket of his pants. Mark hurried to his car and tore through the records, tracing his finger down the list as he scanned the numbers. Two immediately jumped out as suspicious, the first appearing a week before he'd met Vanessa and disappearing around the same time she'd told him she'd blocked Harold's number. The second number popping up a week later was enough to convince him he'd found what he was looking for. After realizing he was blocked, the creep switched to the second number, rendering the first useless. With this in mind, he dialed the second number in hopes Harold would answer. It went straight to voicemail with no ring and no voicemail greeting, leading Mark to believe the phone was shut off. Defeated, he groaned in frustration but took satisfaction in knowing he at least had the number. He wasn't beyond another bribe if it meant getting the name and address attached to it so he could confront the man who'd been harassing her for weeks on end.

On a whim, he called the first number and was surprised when it actually rang. It went to voicemail, and his pulse began to race as he heard Harold's voice for the first time.

"Hello, you've reached Harold Cooper. I'm sorry you missed me, but if you leave your name and number, I'll call you back when I can. Thank you."

Feeling a glimmer of hope for the first time since Vanessa's disappearance, he called Michael McKeever back with his words pouring out before the private investigator could even speak. "Michael, it's Mark again. I got the guy's name and number. I need your help finding an address."

"I'm a little busy right now working another case, Mark. You'll have to give me a bit here. I'm swamped with—"

"Mike, please. Charge me extra. I don't care. Just get me that address."

He relayed Harold Cooper's name along with his number and could hear McKeever jotting it down. "Give me a few, okay? No guarantees."

"Thanks Mike. I'll be here."

Impatient, he sprang from his car and back into the Verizon store. If he had to shell out another five grand to get Harold's information, so be it. It would be a small price to pay to get Vanessa back, hopefully alive and in one piece. He missed her deeply. The way her eyes lit up when she flashed her perfect smile, her laugh, the feeling of her soft lips on his. She actually listened to him, unlike other women who would nod and agree with a vacuous look in their eyes. He'd only known Vanessa for a little over a month, yet he felt like he'd lost his other half. He'd been shaken by the angry voicemail message she'd left him, but her disappearance had completely leveled him. There was no way she'd run away without so much as a word to anyone. The message Harold had sent him the morning after they'd made love for the first time kept replaying in his mind:

*Enjoy her while she lasts, tough guy. She won't be yours long.*

He wished he had done something sooner and had tracked Harold down before he got a chance to take

Vanessa. Dozens of regrets plagued him, keeping him up at night; the dark circles under his eyes were a testament to how sleep-deprived he was. If his love never came back to him, he wondered if he'd ever get a full night of sleep again. Under normal circumstances, he'd have already left for Los Angeles, but he couldn't bring himself to leave with Vanessa missing. He'd apologetically told Zane that their evening workouts would have to wait until she was found since focusing on anything other than her whereabouts was an exercise in and of itself.

Inside the store, the woman was still browsing phones while the young employee stood behind the counter, grinning widely as he typed on his phone. He appeared to be texting somebody, likely boasting about the five thousand dollars he'd just scored.

"Sorry, dude," he said dismissively as Mark approached. "All sales are final. No refunds."

"I don't want my money back," Mark hissed quietly. "This number here," he said, pointing at the number he'd just dialed, "I need the address it belongs to."

"Got some more money for me?" the kid asked, setting his phone aside.

"I just," Mark began to protest loudly but caught himself and lowered his voice. "I just paid you *five thousand* dollars. The least you can do is help me find the address to this number. Come on, man. Work with me here."

The kid sighed but didn't resist. He leaned over the counter and squinted at the number Mark was pointing to, and then typed it into the system. "Sorry, man. It doesn't look like they're a Verizon customer. Can't help."

"Fuck," Mark muttered. He pointed at the second number that had gone directly to voicemail. "What about this one?"

"Not Verizon, either," the kid replied after a search yielded no results.

Mark swallowed his disappointment. "Thank you. You've been a big enough help. I really do appreciate it."

Back in his car, he nervously drummed on the steering wheel with his thumbs, anxiously awaiting word from McKeever. When the call finally came, Mark answered on the first ring.

"Please tell me you found it."

"I think I did. I found an address linked to that phone number in Queens. Down in Jamaica, actually. Have something to write with?"

Mark's hands shook as he took down the address. This was what he'd been waiting for. Since Vanessa's disappearance, he'd envisioned the moment he could finally confront Harold and beat her whereabouts out of him if he had to. Now that he knew where to find him, he wasn't wasting any time. He made his way down through Queens, determined to find the woman he'd fallen so hard for.

The old Ford Tempo in the driveway told him Harold was home when he rolled up on a corner lot at the intersection of Lakeview Boulevard and 122nd Avenue. It was a run-down two-story house and, like the other homes in the rough neighborhood, bars on the windows and a barred screen door added an extra layer of security over the front entrance. The dilapidated porch reminded him of the one he'd grown up with, and a tattered doormat with the word "welcome" barely visible lay crooked under his feet as he steeled himself for a fight. He wasn't leaving this house until he knew what Harold had done with Vanessa, and if that meant spilling blood, he wasn't afraid to get his knuckles messy.

The barred screen door was unlocked, allowing him access to the wooden front door behind it. He refrained from pounding on it, making a conscious effort to knock lightly in fear of scaring Harold off. An aggressive knock might sound like the police and send the loser running out whatever back door there could be. He knocked again, this time slightly louder but not hard enough to raise the alarm. He heard the shuffling of footsteps and a man's voice grumble, "I'm coming, I'm coming."

The door opened a crack, and Mark was greeted by a short, round man with outdated glasses and thinning hair that was lazily combed over. He stood wearing a white t-shirt with noticeable yellowing around the collar and armpits and a pair of gray sweatpants that looked to be in dire need of a wash.

"Harold Cooper?" Mark asked nicely, wanting to make sure he had the right man before getting gruff.

"Yes." Harold looked Mark up and down nervously but didn't seem to recognize him. "Who are you?"

Mark's brow furrowed, and he replied sternly, "You know who I am."

"I-I'm sorry, I think you have the wrong person," Harold stuttered, appearing intimidated by Mark's size and sudden change in demeanor.

"Stop. I know you know who I am, so don't even pretend you don't."

"I've never seen you before. You're confused."

Between the look of sincerity in his eyes and the absence of recognition on his face when he'd first answered the door, Mark was a bit taken aback. It hadn't been the response he'd expected, and it tripped him up for a moment. He held his ground and asked menacingly, "What did you do with Vanessa?"

"Who?" Harold asked, once again looking genuinely confused.

"Don't play dumb, asshole. Vanessa Claire. The girl you've been harassing every goddamn day for weeks now."

"I met a Vanessa online a while back but never knew her last name. It... it didn't go very well. I called her a couple of times and sent her a few text messages but got the hint when she blocked my number. I haven't talked to her since."

"So you're telling me you didn't call or message her from a new number after she blocked you?"

"No, I swear." Harold swallowed hard and asked again, "Who are you?"

Mark had expected to be knocking the man's teeth out by now, but something about the earnest look on his face was stopping him. Either he was a phenomenal actor, or he really didn't know who he was talking to. He'd always heard that sociopaths could be quite manipulative and didn't want to take the chance of failing Vanessa just because Harold had put on a convincing show. If he took the guy at face value and left, he'd never forgive himself if the guy did turn out to be responsible. He had to know for sure.

"Mark Masterson. Vanessa's boyfriend. She's been missing for over a month now, and something tells me you're the reason why."

"Vanessa is missing?"

"That's what I said—enough with the act. You're the only one with a motive. I read the messages you sent her. The ones from your new number after she blocked you."

"New number?" Again, Harold looked completely baffled. "Look, I don't know what you're talking about. I called her and texted her for a week or so after our date, but that's it. I was a dick. I admit it. I'm not proud of that. I was hurt she rejected me, and I said some things I shouldn't have. I haven't talked to her or seen her since."

Mark searched his face for even a glimmer of dishonesty yet saw none. With Harold as the only lead, however, he had no choice but to persist. "I'm not buying it. Here's what I think happened." He inched closer to Harold; muscles tensed, and voiced a low growl in hopes of scaring the man into slipping up. "I think you couldn't handle the rejection. You became obsessed with her. Started following her, following us. Finally, he snapped and hurt her. What did you do with her, Harold?

"Look, I don't know you, and I don't know what happened to that girl," Harold said, backing up a step with a terrified look on his face. "I'm sorry she's missing, but I really can't help. Now please leave."

"I'm not going anywhere until you tell me what you did with her."

"If you don't get off my property, I'm calling the cops."

*Tell me where she is!*" Mark screamed, losing his temper. Lack of sleep combined with Harold's bewildered face as he proclaimed his innocence was just too much for him. He snapped, unable to control himself as his anger consumed him. Harold jumped in fright and tried to shut the door, but Mark pushed it open with ease. Stepping into the house, he grabbed the man by the neck and slammed him to the floor hard, sending his glasses flying from his face. "Where is she?"

*"Please, mister, I don't know!"* Harold cried, shielding his face with his hands. "I didn't touch her, I swear. Please, just leave me alone!"

Mark kneeled over the man, one hand wrapped around his throat and the other raised in a fist. "You want to do this the hard way, huh? I'll beat the shit out of you until you start talking!"

A pleading voice interrupted out of nowhere. "Please! Please don't hurt my boy! He's all I got!"

Mark looked up to see an older woman staring at him in horror. Barely able to stand, she was supporting herself with a wobbly cane, her wispy hair thin and grey. She looked frail and weak, her eyes filling with tears at the sight of Mark's fist hovering above Harold's face.

"M-mom," Harold sputtered, casting her a worried glance. "Go back to your room."

Mark looked at his raised fist, then at the terrified woman struggling just to stand. The thought of somebody other than Harold—and possibly Vanessa— being in the house had never crossed his mind. Not only was there another person, but that other person was Harold's mother, who was clearly suffering from some illness. An illness that, if judged by looks alone, appeared to be terminal. He was suddenly overcome with guilt, ashamed that he'd just assaulted this man in front of his own mother. He lowered his hand and released his grip on Harold's neck.

"I'm sorry," he told the woman, smoothing out his suit and adjusting his tie. "Your son and I just had a little misunderstanding, that's all."

She eyed him skeptically as she shook. "Who are you, and why are you in my house?"

"Mom, its okay," Harold said, reaching for his glasses and rising to his feet. He rushed to her side and threw her arm over his shoulder to help support her. "Let's get you back to bed."

Mark watched as Harold guided her down the hall and into what he could only presume to be a bedroom. He didn't follow, choosing to give them the privacy they needed. Unsure if Harold would return with a weapon of some sort, perhaps a gun, he looked at the open front door and debated leaving. He took a step toward it but couldn't bring himself to go. It was a two-story house with plenty of places for Harold to stash

Vanessa. He came here resolute on finding her and couldn't leave until he did.

Harold returned a moment later, cautiously keeping his distance. He took a deep breath and let it out heavily. "Cancer."

"I'm sorry," Mark replied. Conflicting emotions ran through him. He found himself feeling sorry for the man who'd been tasked with taking care of his dying mother. He also wanted to finish what he'd started, pummeling Harold until he told him where to find Vanessa. That option was off the table, though. He couldn't hurt a sick woman's son in front of her.

"She's really upset," Harold said. "I think you should leave. I won't call the cops."

"I wish I could do that, but I can't. I love her. I need to find her."

"Well, you're not going to find her here. I know I can be a dick sometimes, but I'd never hurt anybody. I'm bad with women. That doesn't make me a kidnapper, or killer, or whatever it is you think I am."

Mark stood in contemplation for a moment before speaking. "If you're really innocent, you wouldn't mind letting me take a look around this place."

"If that's what it'll take to get you out of here, then knock yourself out," Harold grumbled.

From the top down, Mark made his way through the cluttered house, looking for Vanessa or any signs that she'd been there. With how full of junk the place was, he couldn't imagine there being any room to keep anybody hostage. The attic was packed with boxes and old furniture, as were the three upstairs bedrooms. It was obvious from the degree of useless stuff that Harold or his mother had a problem with hoarding. He suspected it was both. There was barely room to walk, let alone stash a living person. The house was also filthy, with evidence of rodents and insects everywhere. The bathroom was so disgusting he didn't dare step foot in it, but it was so small he didn't have to. One quick peek was all he needed to know. She wasn't in there and likely hadn't been.

"I haven't had much time to clean," Harold told him, looking embarrassed. He'd been following behind Mark as he explored the place, hoping to find any trace of Vanessa.

Downstairs, Mark made a point not to disturb Harold's resting mother as he continued to snoop. He poked his head into her room for a brief look before searching the remaining bedroom and bathroom. Both were a cluttered, dirty mess, but neither of them held any clues.

"Happy?" Harold asked, ushering Mark toward the front door.

"Not until I check the basement."

Harold cast a nervous glance at the door leading down to the basement. For the first time during their encounter, he finally looked guilty.

*Gotcha*, Mark thought.

# Chapter Fifteen
## *Vanessa*

Instigating the fight with Harold had proven to be a very dumb move. She had to do it, though. She had to push his buttons to see what he was capable of. In testing him, she'd learned that he didn't have the nerve to lay his hands on her. Either he was a coward or cared about her too much to cause her any real harm. She suspected it was a combination of both, with a sprinkling of fear. Fear that she would retaliate and possibly overcome him physically. Yes, he had finally raised a hand to her after she'd continued to provoke him, but it had been a laughable attempt at a strike that showed he wasn't a fighter. He was also woefully out of shape. That much was evident from how hard he'd be breathing just from walking up and down the basement stairs. She could see his chest heaving slightly and hear his wheezing through the stupid goat mask he never went without.

The man seemed determined to win her over, which surely played a role in his refusal to harm her. Sure, he had abducted her and locked her in a basement. She hated him for that. Yet, she was also aware that he hadn't taken advantage of her. Aside from stripping her naked to put the robe on her, he'd never touched her inappropriately. He could have been forcing himself on her every day, but he hadn't. When he told her that he only wanted her of her own volition, he seemed to have meant it.

Squaring off with him had been a dangerous game. He could have killed her, and nobody would have ever known, but she'd proven that he wasn't aggressive enough to hurt her. The only physical pain he'd caused her was during the abduction, and that had been with a Taser—the weapon of choice for somebody who doesn't want to cause lasting, long-term damage. It was the ideal method for incapacitating her without getting his hands dirty and, in her opinion, confirmed his cowardice. Most men would have tossed her around like a rag doll and choked her out, but Harold was too gentle for that, just like most captors would have cleaned her clock for mouthing off to them rather than sulking out of the room like a child.

Instead of violence, Harold had found other ways of punishing her for her defiance. In the week since their scuffle, he'd cut her food down to one meal a day and had been shutting the light off at night, leaving her alone in the dark. After a couple of nights, she'd adjusted to that and found it didn't bother her as much as she'd thought it would. Without his voice changer, their evening chats had ceased. If he considered that a form of punishment, he was sorely mistaken. In fact, since smashing the device, he hadn't said a single word to her, which she'd been just fine with. He'd communicate using hand gestures and grunts, something she much preferred over the poorly digitized voice he'd been using.

No, the real torment had come in the form of pictures. The morning following her outburst, he'd slid her meal across the floor along with a manila folder. In it, she'd found a variety of nude photos that he'd taken when she was still unconscious from the chloroform. He'd told her that he hadn't touched her, but he'd neglected to mention the large number of pictures he'd taken while she was passed out. It looked as if he'd printed them from home using an inkjet printer. She'd burst into tears at the sight of them, the same sense of violation returning that she'd felt when she'd first discovered he'd stripped her nude. One of them depicted his rather small cock in her face, but it didn't appear to actually be touching her. She'd torn the pictures into small pieces, scattering them across the basement floor where they still lay.

By now, she'd accepted that she wouldn't be rescued. If her count was correct, she'd been trapped in his basement for almost forty days and was still no closer to free. How the cops hadn't questioned Harold yet was beyond her. Maybe they had and had somehow written him off as a suspect. She found that hard to believe, given how unstable the guy was. Any detective worth his weight would have picked up on the weird vibe he put out and investigated further. Somebody would have poked around his house already. Being a struggling black woman from Brooklyn with few friends and little family, she feared she wasn't a priority and her case would get lost among the others. She imagined her paperwork being shoved into a filing cabinet and forgotten, leaving her stuck in this room for the rest of her life.

The thought of months going by filled her with despair. The thought of years going by was almost too much to bear. What if Harold's plan worked? Hell, it had been working so far. Developing an attachment to him seemed absurd now, but after years of relying on him for everything—shelter, food, water—it wasn't beyond the realm of possibility. He controlled every facet of her life down here in this musty, lonely basement. She'd seen and heard stories of captives who eventually broke down, becoming completely subservient to their captors. They all had the same faraway look in their eyes as if they'd been drained of their very being. It was almost a form of brainwashing, forcing a person to become so reliant on you that they surrender their mind and body. She feared years of captivity could break her spirit and didn't want to stick around long enough to find out.

The pictures Harold had taunted her with were her breaking point. After ripping them into confetti and spraying them everywhere, she vowed to escape or die trying. She didn't have many options since he'd done such a good job securing her and limiting any possible weapons, but she began crafting a plan she thought might work. Every day, he fed her on the same ceramic plate that, if broken in just the right way, might leave a fragment big enough to use as a shiv. If she could break the plate and somehow get him close enough, she might be able to stab him with a piece of it. She'd seen it done on a television show, though rather unsuccessfully, but it was the only shot she had.

Also weighing on her mind was the period she'd missed. She was two weeks late now, which certainly wasn't normal for her. Her cycle was usually like clockwork, making the missed period cause for mild alarm. She'd fallen so hard for Mark that she'd never bothered with protection, which she freely admitted was stupid. Love, it seemed, made smart people do very dumb things, often overriding logic. Casting a look around the dank basement, she wondered if Harold's love for her was why he'd made the irrational decision to abduct her. She scolded herself for the thought and corrected herself. Harold wasn't in love with her… he was obsessed with her.

The missed period didn't mean she was pregnant, of course. She was well aware that the stress of her captivity could have thrown her cycle off. If she was pregnant, however, that didn't bode well, as Harold surely hadn't signed on to care for another man's baby. There was no telling what he might do. It might be enough for him to scrap his entire plan and end her life with an overdose of the remaining chloroform or some other cowardly way. He didn't have the stomach to use his hands, let alone a knife or a gun; that much she'd established already. At the very least, he'd get rid of the child, and that thought alone scared her more than anything. She considered hiding the possible pregnancy from him but deemed it pointless since he'd find out eventually if she was. Instead, she chose to weave it into her plan, using it to lower his guard long enough for her to strike.

He'd been feeding her one meal before leaving for work in the morning and retrieving the plate when he got home. She'd pick at it throughout the day, trying to make it last since she wasn't sure how long her punishment was going to continue. The daily meal wasn't even enough to sustain her, let alone a developing baby. She'd lost a few pounds over the week, the chain around her waist noticeably looser but still unable to be squeezed out of. If she was going to escape, she wasn't going to wait any longer. Today was going to be the day.

She clenched her abdomen and rocked back and forth in mock pain as Harold shuffled in with her breakfast. He slid it across the floor to her in his usual fashion, and then took a step back, eyeing her discomfort through his mask.

"H-Harold…" she groaned. "I-I don't feel well. I'm sick."

He stood watching her for a moment before turning to leave.

"I think I'm pregnant," she blurted, stopping him. He shot back around, staring at her again in silence. If she could see his face, she was certain it was painted with a mixture of anger and concern.

She snatched the bucket from the end of her bed and pretended to puke. "S-something's wrong. I need help."

He slammed his foot down hard in outrage and bolted out of the room, locking the basement up behind him. She cocked her head and listened, hearing the front door slam loudly as he stormed out of the house. She'd anticipated that reaction but hadn't anticipated him returning fifteen minutes later with an at-home pregnancy test. He threw it onto the cot and worked his hand under his mask to cover his mouth.

"Take it," he said through gritted teeth, his lowered voice muffled by his hand. They were the first words he'd spoken without the voice changer. Given how clever he'd proven himself to be, she'd begun to wonder if the mask and voice changer weren't just a way to disassociate himself from the crime he'd committed but were a way for him to defend himself should he get caught. With them, he could claim his innocence by pointing out that she'd never seen his face or heard his voice. Therefore, she couldn't prove he was her abductor. That seemed outlandish, but it was a move she could see Harold pulling. Smashing his voice changer was a step toward identifying him when and if the day came. The second step was getting that ridiculous mask off.

"What?" she asked, grabbing the bucket and feigning sickness again.

Again, the low, muffled growl. "Take the test."

"Right now? In front of you?"

He nodded yes and stood, waiting. He'd watched her clean her naked body numerous times, but peeing in front of him was where she drew the line.

"No. At least let me be a lady. Give me that, please."

He sighed in frustration and left the room. With her back to the door, she ripped the pregnancy test open and glanced over her shoulder to make sure he wasn't peeking in. She untied the robe and let it drape by her sides as she squatted over the bucket with the test between her legs. She hadn't expected him to run out and buy a pregnancy test but was glad he did so she could know for sure. This was important to her, and it was obviously important to him since he was now running late for work because of it.

"Finished," she called after squeezing out what she could.

He stepped back into the room and gestured for her to show him the results.

"It takes a minute," she told him, staring at the test.

He paced the floor, agitated and impatient but staying out of her reach. She watched as two pink lines slowly appeared on the strip, erasing any doubts of her pregnancy. Hesitant to tell him in fear of what he might do, her voice trembled as she told him, "I-I'm... pregnant."

He lost it. Releasing a loud roar, he kicked his metal folding chair into the wall, then picked it up and threw it onto the concrete floor, leaving it a bent mess. Dropping to his knees, he brought his hands to his head, and, for a moment, she thought he was going to take his mask off. He remained there with his hands holding his head in distress, and she could tell by his slumped, hitching shoulders that he was crying.

"Harold?" she asked gently after a minute had passed. Clenching her abdomen and pretending to be in pain again, she continued, "I think something's wrong with the baby. I need to go to the hospital. Please... you have to let me go now."

He slowly returned to his feet and composed himself. Just outside the door was the broom handle with the bent coat hanger attached to it that he'd been using to collect her plate and bucket every day. Reaching for it, he studied the coat hanger for a moment. He looked at her, and then looked back at the coat hanger, adjusting it slightly while she watched in horror.

"Oh my God," she muttered, slowly backing up and beginning to sob. "Oh… oh my God, no. Harold, no. No!"

"Tonight," he hissed.

He slammed the door and locked it, leaving her in tears. She collapsed on the cot, her body shaking as she wailed. She knew what Harold was going to try to do, and she wasn't going to let it happen. She needed to pull herself together and stick to her plan if there was any chance of keeping her baby and possibly her life. Drying her eyes, she waited for Harold to leave the house and set to work, removing another small spring from the cot that she then bent straight. After scattering her food on the floor, she began scoring the shape of a long triangle into the plate with the thin piece of metal. She repeatedly traced the shape, slowly carving the outline of it into the ceramic. If she did it right, dropping the plate would leave the long triangle she'd cut, giving her an effective weapon to use against Harold.

Knowing she only had one shot, she traced the shape a few more times until she felt the groove she'd made was deep enough.

She held the plate a few feet off of the concrete floor and took a deep breath. This was it—the moment of truth. Dropping the plate, she watched as it shattered, leaving a large piece in the shape of a long triangle. It had worked. She picked the piece up and practiced with it, making sure she knew how to hold it so she could deliver the perfect strike. To make sure it was sharp enough to do serious damage, she ground it to a fine point using the concrete floor. When she was confident in the makeshift knife she'd created, she set it on the cot beside her to begin the waiting game. Harold was in for a big surprise when he came home.

With hours to kill, she nodded in and out of sleep while thinking about Mark, something she'd been doing often. She knew she shouldn't, but he had treated her well, despite his lies, by making her feel special. He'd burst into genuine laughter at her jokes, listen to her stories with earnest interest, and take a sincere fascination in her hopes and dreams. The energy between them had been real. He had deceived her, but he hadn't been able to fake their connection. Making things harder was not only how gorgeous he was but how incredible the sex had been. He'd touched her in ways no man ever had and probably wouldn't be able to again. It was hard not to miss him, even though he'd made a fool of her. If she made it out of this, she was going to have to talk to him since she was carrying his child. If her plan failed, however, she might not be carrying the child much longer.

With Harold bound to return soon, she pushed Mark from her mind to go over her plan again. She was taking a few more practice jabs with her shiv when she heard the creaking of the floorboards above her. Heart beating fast, she dropped to the floor facing the cot, the scattered food and remaining pieces of the broken plate lying by her side. She'd staged the scene to look as if she'd dropped her plate of food while collapsing from her imaginary ailment, a ploy to get Harold close enough to drive the makeshift knife she was concealing into whatever part of him she could. She had the shiv tucked under her side, hidden from his view yet easily accessible should he step near her.

Vanessa heard the familiar sound of Harold's keys jingling as he unlocked the door. Adrenaline surging, she tried her best to remain still as she felt him looking her over.

"Get up," she heard him say, using the same technique he had that morning.

She remained motionless, her hand on the triangle fragment by her side.

"Get up," he repeated louder, his teeth still gritted and voice lowered.

She'd planted the idea in his head hours earlier that she hadn't been feeling well. The unexpected pregnancy test, which turned out positive, was a lucky break that lent credibility to her story. There was a good chance he'd think that complications from the pregnancy were responsible for her sickness and lower his defenses.

"Vanessa?" he asked, continuing to disguise his voice. A minute went by with no sound from him, making her nervous. Laying on her side with her back to him, she couldn't see what he was doing even if she dared to peek. Her heart pounded as she waited. A sudden poke at her side told her he was using the broom handle to nudge her.

"Come on. Get up."

She held the shard of the plate tighter as she sensed his approach. He poked her side with the handle again and waited a few seconds. Then, another poke.

"Vanessa?"

Yet another poke. She heard the sound of the broom handle gently hitting the concrete floor, strewn with food and pieces of her shredded photos, and knew he'd set it down.

Finally, she felt his hand on her shoulder and could feel him kneeling next to her.

"Vanessa?"

In one fluid movement, she rolled over and drove the shiv into his shoulder as hard as she could. He shrieked in pain and tried to back away, but she grabbed him by his shirt and pulled him toward her, stabbing him again in the gut and lodging the shiv there. He let out another loud shriek and fell to his knees, clenching his stomach as blood poured from the wound. She seized the chance to wrap the chain around his neck and stood behind him with her knee pressed into his back, pulling hard while he fought to escape.

*"Fuck you!"* she growled, her face twisted in anger. *"Just die already!"*

He clawed at the metal links with both hands while blood continued to gush from the two deep gashes. Horrible wheezes and croaks escaped him as he struggled to breathe, but she didn't let up, mustering all of her strength to pull harder until he went limp. She pulled on the chain again to make sure he was really out, then released it and watched his body crumple to the floor.

She stood over him, breathing heavily from the effort it had taken to strangle him. Blood pooled by his side and mixed with the remnants of the photos she'd torn to pieces. Her hands shook from the adrenaline still surging through her as she knelt down to retrieve the keys. They weren't in his left pocket, so she rolled him over to try the other, which wasn't easy given his extra weight. In moving him, he released a long, low groan through the goat mask, revealing he was still alive. She dug into his right pocket and pulled out the keys, scrambling to find the one she needed. There was no guarantee the padlock keys were even on the small keychain, but luck was on her side again. Two small keys, similar in size and shape, presented themselves, and the second did the trick, unlocking the padlock on her waist and freeing her of the chain.

She tossed the keys aside and ran for the basement door but stopped before hitting the stairs. Breathing hard from the rush of her success, she turned to face Harold. He'd regained consciousness and lay bleeding, his hand on his side as he writhed in pain.

"H-h-help me..." he groaned in a voice that sounded vaguely familiar.

Without an ounce of sympathy for the man, she returned to his side and watched as he bled, looking up at her through the lifeless eyes of his mask. He pleaded with her again, and she replied with a swift kick to his face. He yelped as his head flew to the side, his mask twisting but not coming off. Food, blood, and tiny pieces of the pictures she'd shredded were stuck to it, and she could see the thin rubber material moving from his short, labored breaths. After forty days of staring at that mask, an almost maniacal grin painted her face as she bent down to tear it off his head. His hands moved from his wounded gut to his mask, and he made a feeble attempt to hold it over his face. With one quick tug, she pulled it off, finally revealing Harold's face. Only... it wasn't Harold. It was Doug.

She froze, unable to process what she was seeing. It was as if her mind had completely seized, briefly robbing her of her motor skills. Her jaw fell open, and she stared at the face of her best friend, his pained eyes looking back at her with guilt. She dropped to her knees and began to sob, desperately trying to make sense of what was happening.

"V-Vanessa..." he spoke with an apologetic look, reaching out to her for help. "Please."

In the five weeks she'd been held prisoner, the thought of anyone other than Harold being her abductor hadn't crossed her mind. She was so certain it was him she hadn't even considered other possibilities. Her supposed best friend being responsible simply didn't make sense, and a thousand different thoughts flooded her as she wrestled to understand what was happening.

"Doug, what the fuck?" she cried, lips trembling and tears streaming down her cheeks. "Why? Why, Doug?"

He rolled onto his side, wincing in agony, and managed to work himself into a seated position with his back resting on the cot. He screamed in pain, legs flailing as he pulled the shard of the plate from his gut and tossed it onto the floor.

"You got me good," he said, looking down at his bleeding shoulder. His hands were covering his wounded gut, more blood seeping from between his fingers. "Well played."

She watched, still unable to move, as he managed to pull the pillow from her bed and removed its pillowcase, pressing it to his wounded gut in an effort to stop the bleeding. He tried rising to his feet but couldn't quite manage. Sitting back down, his chest hitched as he rode out the pain.

"You're sick," she told him, shaking her head in disgust. "All this time… all this time, I thought you were Harold. How could you do this to me? You were my friend, Doug!"

When he closed his eyes, she wasn't sure if it was from the pain or the shame of what he'd done. Tears began to escape as he replied, "I've been in love with you since the first moment I saw you. Three years ago, almost to the day." He smiled as if reliving a memory. "You were the prettiest thing I'd ever seen. You still are."

"But… you're gay," she said, looking at him questioningly.

"What the fuck?" he fired back, eyes shooting open and locking on to her angrily. "You thought I was gay?"

"You're telling me you're not?" She knew she should be running out the door and making her escape, yet she couldn't tear herself away from him. She had to know why he'd done such a cruel thing after three years of friendship. She needed some sort of an explanation.

*"Of course I'm not!"* He began to cough and turned his head, spitting blood onto the floor. She wasn't sure if he was bleeding internally or if it had been from her kick to his face. "How could you even think that?"

"Uh, have you listened to the way you speak?"

"So I don't have the manliest voice," he shrugged. "That makes me gay?"

"Doug… you crochet and have cats."

He rolled his eyes. "I don't fucking crochet, Vanessa. That stuff upstairs is my mom's. I only told you that so you'd think we had something in common." He paused and added, "I don't even like cats. I got them because I knew you did."

"Jesus, that's fucked up." She probed him further in horrified curiosity. "But… you never even talked about women. Like, ever."

"Why would I? You're the only woman I've wanted. The second I met you, I knew I'd never want anybody else."

Her mind reeled as she tried to make sense of everything. With his admissions, the pieces quickly began to fit, and she felt her stomach turn at the realization of how manipulated she'd been. He'd worked himself into the role of best friend by feigning her same likes and interests as a way to get close to her. Mark's deception, as hurtful as it had been, paled in comparison to Doug's.

"You're... you're not right in the head." She swallowed hard, still trying to grasp this devastating revelation. Her reality had been turned upside down the moment she'd torn the mask off his head. "You lied to me. Lied to me about everything."

"I'm so sorry, Vanessa. I... I had to."

"You had to?" she spat bitterly.

"Look at me." He removed a hand from the pillowcase, now soaked in blood, and motioned to his body. "I'm short. Fat. Ugly. White. We're total opposites. You would have never given a guy like me the time of day."

"So, what, you just decided to lie your way into my life?"

"I was hoping if you just got to know me, you'd give me a chance. Instead, you friend-zoned me. Let's be honest here. There was no chance of me getting out of that. You knew it, and I knew it."

Rising to her feet, she inched away from him while shaking her head. "Yeah, well, now you're going to prison for a very long time."

"Vanessa, don't..." he reached out to her, but she was finished with him. She'd heard all she needed to. Springing up the stairs, she burst into his living room through a door she'd always assumed led to a closet. In the three years she'd known him, he'd never shown her the basement, and she'd had no reason to venture down there.

The ugly, plaid couch greeted her, and she felt a twang of pain as memories of their movie nights came rushing back to her. Who knew how many of them he'd spent sitting next to her while fantasizing about locking her in the basement right below their feet? She cringed at the thought and rushed to the front door, only to find it secured from the inside by not only one but three separate locks. Knowing the small house didn't have a back door, she hurried to the nearest window but found it boarded shut, as were the others. It seemed as if Doug had made contingency plans for if she'd escaped the basement.

She'd foolishly left the keychain downstairs, thinking she no longer needed it. With Doug incapacitated from his wounds and no longer a threat, she rushed back down the stairs, hoping the remaining keys were to the three locks on the front door. Before she could fully register his absence from the side of the cot, something hard came crashing down on her head, sending her sprawling onto the floor.

"Forget something?" Doug smirked, dangling the keys. In his other hand was the dented metal folding chair he'd kicked around that morning. He'd managed to fold it back up and had used it as a weapon, hitting her so hard she was now seeing two of him.

"How..." she began, trailing off as the room started to fade.

"I might not have been in as much pain as I let on," he replied with an evil grin.

Fighting to stay conscious, she rolled onto her side and attempted to get on her feet. She failed rather spectacularly while Doug watched, laughing. "Not so tough now, are we?"

The Doug from just a few minutes earlier, who'd seemed remorseful and scared, was long gone. He was now cruel and vindictive, taking pleasure in her pain.

There was a warm, wet feeling on the back of her head that she knew was blood before her fingers even confirmed it. Thinking she may have a concussion, she tried her hardest to stay awake but felt herself slipping. She succumbed, briefly passing out and waking with the chain locked around her waist again. In her haste to flee the scene, she'd allowed herself to slip up; making a crucial mistake that had landed her back in Doug's control.

"Doug," she groaned, still on the floor where she'd fallen. With his wounds, Doug likely didn't have the strength to move her back to the cot. Looking around the room, she realized he was no longer there. She slipped into darkness again and awoke sometime later with him seated in the bent folding chair just outside her reach.

"Well, look who's awake," he smiled.

"Doug… my head…"

"Oh, does your head hurt?" he mocked. "Gee, I'm sorry. You know what really hurts? The huge gouges in my shoulder and stomach."

He'd changed into an unflatteringly tight gray t-shirt, and she could see the outline of bandages underneath. He'd patched himself up, but with how deep the wounds had been, she didn't think he'd heal without actual medical assistance. She could see a thin layer of sweat on his brow, and his breathing was still labored, indicating he was in quite a bit of pain. Thoughts of him dying and leaving her chained in the basement to waste away and rot flashed through her mind.

"It's over, Doug," she told him. "Just let me go now. We both need to go to the hospital."

"Yeah, that's not going to happen," he laughed. Sensing her concern, he added, "Don't worry, I'm not going to die on you."

"You will if you don't get those wounds taken care of."

He shrugged, his hand holding his injured side. "Eh. If I do, I do. And if I do, you do. Maybe then we can finally be together."

"You realize how crazy that sounds, right?" She managed to get on her feet and staggered to the cot, avoiding the blood and food on the floor.

"Had you just given me a chance, none of this would be happening? You drove me to it."

"Don't you dare blame me for this," she huffed, sitting on the cot and feeling the knot on the back of her head. Her hair was matted in dried blood.

"I gave you every opportunity, Vanessa. I was an open door. I always told you I was the only man you needed. You can't tell me you didn't see the way I looked at you."

"I… I seriously thought you were gay."

He rolled his head and groaned in frustration. "Will you stop with that? Sorry I'm not some muscle-bound alpha male douchebag like that billionaire you—"

She could tell he hadn't meant to vocalize that last part. He looked away, realizing what he'd said. In his anger, the words had just come pouring out.

"Billionaire? What are you talking about?" When he didn't say anything, she asked again. "Doug? What are you talking about?"

"Mark!" he blurted. "He's not the manager of that gym. He owns the entire chain. You think you're so smart, but you never figured that out. I figured it out in, like, a day."

"Only because you were stalking him, too," she pointed out.

"Stalking? No. Just trying to learn his weaknesses so I could exploit them."

"And?"

He let out a long sigh and admitted, "The guy has none. It's like he's perfect or something. I told you earlier, there's no way I could compete with that."

She recalled the video of Mark kissing his wife and two kids. She'd received it the last movie night she'd had with Doug. He'd excused himself to the bathroom after seeming annoyed by her affection for Mark, and the message had conveniently come through while he was in there.

"Doug... did you send me that video?" She swallowed nervously, already knowing the answer.

"You're goddamn right I did. I had to do something to pry you off that guy's dick. You really didn't leave me any other choice."

Vanessa's mind reeled again at the confirmation it had been Doug harassing her from the second phone number. All those weeks, he'd been the one bombarding her with messages, not Harold. It was all a big game to him. She knew there was more he wasn't telling her. She was almost afraid to ask but had to know. "Were those really his wife and kids?"

He looked guilty as he avoided eye contact, pressing his hand to the bandage on his shoulder. When he didn't answer, she asked again. "Doug? Were those really his wife and kids?"

"I guess it doesn't matter if you know," he sighed. "It's not like you're getting out of here. That was his sister and nephews."

That revelation stung hard. She'd completely flown off the handle, ending things with him through a voicemail before offering him the chance to explain. She did recall Mark briefly mentioning a sister and telling her about his two nephews. Yet, Doug had coaxed her into believing he was married with kids, and she hadn't even questioned it. She couldn't help but feel stupid.

"So let me get this straight. He's rich, and he's not married?"

"Ding, ding, ding," Doug replied sarcastically, ringing an imaginary bell.

"You couldn't just let me be happy. You had to ruin everything," she growled.

"I could have made you happy, but you chose a guy with money and looks. Funny, I never took you for a shallow bitch."

"We had a connection you and I never had, Doug." She felt her face getting warm, a sign of the rage building up inside of her. If she hadn't been locked up again, she would be tearing the smug look off of his face.

"We had a connection. I know we did. I felt it. It was real."

"No, Doug, it wasn't. You're insane."

"I can't believe you're pregnant with his baby," he scoffed. "Shallow and a whore."

She recalled Harold calling her a whore in the coffee shop all those weeks earlier. The word had always been one of her few triggers, but she swallowed her anger, trying not to explode since it would do her no good. "If I'm such a shallow whore, why not just let me go?"

"Because you weren't always a shallow whore. Mark turned you into one. I can turn you back. I know I can. It's just… it's going to take time."

"Somebody will find me," she insisted. "It's just a matter of time."

Doug threw his head back and released a laugh that turned into a cough. He winced and held his side. "Not likely. The police called me in for questioning a couple of weeks ago, you know. I'm the last person they suspect."

"They'll come around to you again. They're not idiots."

"You sure about that?" He smiled wide, and his shoulders hitched as he chuckled. "Get this… they think Mark killed you."

"What?" she gasped. "Why would they think that?"

"Because that's what I told them. Thanks to me, they think Mark has a violent temper that you set off when you broke up with him. Damn, I'm good."

She mulled over the idea for a moment. "No. No, they'll realize it wasn't him and come for you."

"Nah. If anything, they'll move on to Harold before giving up completely."

"If they find him through my phone records, they'll find you, too."

He pulled a cell phone from his pocket and held it up. "Pre-paid. Untraceable. Again, I'm smarter than you give me credit for. Maybe someday you'll learn to appreciate just how smart I am. Maybe it'll be one of the things you love about me."

"Are you listening to yourself? Just let me go. This little long-term plan of yours isn't going to work."

"You're right. It's not going to work. Not with you pregnant. I'll be taking care of that as soon as I'm healed up, don't you worry."

Her jaw trembled. "You're not taking my baby."

"Either the baby goes, or you both go. It's that simple."

"Doug…"

"If you ever have a baby, it will be ours," he said, groaning in pain as he stood to leave. "When you fall in love with me."

*I hope you die, you piece of shit!"* she screamed, releasing all of her anger.

"Sleep tight," he smirked, shutting off the light and leaving her alone in the cold, dark basement.

# Chapter Sixteen

## *Mark*

*Gotcha*, Mark thought as a visibly nervous Harold watched him open the door. He made his way down the old wooden stairs into a basement that seemed to serve as Harold's private space. The floor had been covered with a large area rug. Shelves of vinyl albums lined the walls, and in the middle of the room, a record player sat on an end table situated next to a recliner that had seen better days. An older model television with a DVD player seated on top of it was positioned in the corner of the room, a mini-fridge by its side. There was no sign of Vanessa, but Mark did uncover the source of Harold's nervousness, which he now recognized as an embarrassment. Stored under the basement stairs were boxes of pornography overflowing with videos and magazines of all sorts.

"It gets lonely down here sometimes," Harold, muttered, avoiding Mark's judging eyes.

"Sure," Mark replied, peeking into a box that contained a deflated sex doll. "Jesus."

"Don't tell my mother."

"Your secret's safe with me."

After another quick look around the basement, Mark sighed in defeat, knowing Vanessa hadn't been here or anywhere else in the house, for that matter.

"Now, are you happy?" Harold asked, looking annoyed.

Mark wouldn't be happy until he found Vanessa, but he had no reason to hold the man up any longer. He trudged back up the stairs and thanked him for allowing him to look around while continuing to eye him suspiciously. Harold wasn't off the hook yet. Just because Vanessa didn't appear to have been in the house, that didn't mean the guy wasn't responsible. He could have stashed her somewhere else or killed her on a whim, disposing of her body long ago. Still, he couldn't shake the feeling that Harold was being truthful.

He'd come looking for answers but found himself leaving with only questions. If Harold wasn't lying, who took Vanessa? He pulled away from Harold's house and parked down the street to sift through the possibilities. Vanessa didn't seem irrational enough to do something stupid, like disappear somewhere to hurt herself or hide. The abrupt ending to the voicemail she'd left had led him to believe she was attacked mid-sentence. It was true that she didn't live in the best neighborhood, so an assault by a stranger wasn't beyond the realm of possibility. Even with that, a nagging feeling told him it wasn't a random abduction.

He reached into his passenger seat for the folder of information McKeever had given him. In it were as many details as the private investigator had been able to dig up on the few people in Vanessa's social circle. She had a couple of female friends she didn't talk to very often, let alone see, and Daryl, her ex-boyfriend, had moved to Chicago a year earlier to shack up with his new girl. The only person she'd spent much time with over the last three years was Doug, her best friend, whom she suspected was gay. If she had any other friends or enemies they hadn't been clued into yet, Doug might be the only one who knew about them. It was a long shot, but it was worth asking the guy about. He pulled Doug's address from the folder and started in his direction. Along the way, he called Michael McKeever again to let him know what had transpired.

"Mike, hey, it's Mark Masterson again. I just met our guy, Harold. Either he's an amazing actor, or he has no idea where Vanessa is. I searched his house. No sign of her."

"Interesting," McKeever replied. "Still doesn't mean he's innocent."

"I know, I know. He claims he never got a new number and seemed pretty convincing. I need you to look up this second number for me if you can. See who the carrier is. If I have to grease another palm, I'm fine with that."

He read McKeever the number from Vanessa's phone records and waited while the investigator looked into it. McKeever was good. It didn't take long.

"It's a burner phone. Pre-paid. Can't be traced."

"Shit."

"Sorry. If you need anything else, try to wait until tomorrow. I really have to finish up this other case I'm working on."

"I know, I know. I apologize for being such a pain."

"It's okay. If it were my girl, I'm sure I'd be no better."

He ended the call as he continued to Doug's address in lower Brooklyn. Like Harold's place, it was a corner lot that was more recessed from the road. The only neighboring house sat vacant with a crooked for sale sign posted at the end of the driveway. The sun had set an hour earlier, yet Mark couldn't see any light coming from inside Doug's small, one-story home. A car was parked in the driveway, leading him to believe the guy was there, but it seemed too early for him to have gone to bed. There was no porch, just a concrete stoop with three steps that he quickly made his way up. The only light he could detect was coming through the small peephole in the front door, but that meant there was at least one light inside the house. That made no sense to him since the windows were all dark. Leaning over to look at the front window nearest him, he noticed it appeared to have been boarded over, which seemed odd. He knocked on the door and heard a faint scuffling, then saw the light from the peephole go black as somebody, presumably Doug, checked to see who was outside.

Doug cracked the door, looking disheveled, something that seemed out of character for him. Mark had only met him twice, yet he'd been dressed quite nicely and seemed to take a degree of pride in his appearance. He stood with messy hair, wearing black pants, black boots, and a gray t-shirt that seemed a size too small. His face looked pale, and his sunken eyes had an edginess to them.

"Oh, hi, Mark!" he greeted, a bit too enthusiastically. "I wasn't expecting you."

"Are you okay?" Mark asked, looking him over.

"Me? I'm fine. I mean, I'm feeling a little under the weather, but I'll be okay. What's up?"

He spoke quickly with a fake smile on his face that Mark found unsettling. He knew the guy didn't like him, so the forced pleasantness was strange. In the two times Mark had interacted with him, Doug had been cold and curt.

"Sorry to stop by unannounced like this. I just thought you should know that I tracked down Harold."

"You did?' Doug asked, flashing a brief glimpse of nervousness. He stood in the cracked doorway, blocking Mark's view of the inside.

"Yeah. We had a little chat. I even searched his house. I hate to say it… but I'm not so sure the guy did it."

A cat appeared by Doug's foot to investigate who was at the door. Mark was surprised when he callously kicked it out of the way. "Really? That's weird. Are you sure? I mean, it has to be him, right?"

Mark noticed a dark spot forming on Doug's lower stomach. Through the tight shirt, he could see the faint outline of what appeared to be a rectangle. It was a bandage, and the spot forming was blood.

"Are you bleeding?" he asked with concern, pointing at Doug's gut.

Doug looked down and noticed the growing stain. "Oh, um, yeah, I had my appendix taken out. It's not healing very well."

"I'm pretty sure it shouldn't be bleeding. Let me give you a ride to the hospital," Mark offered.

"No! No… I'm good. I'll drive myself if it gets worse. Thank you, though."

Mark thought he saw the outline of another bandage on Doug's shoulder, but he couldn't be sure.

"It's really no problem. It's on my way home anyway, so it—"

"I'm fine, really," Doug interrupted again with his fake smile. "Did you need something, or…?"

"Actually, yes. Since you knew Vanessa best, I was hoping you could point me in another direction. Maybe somebody who had a grudge? There has to be someone we're not thinking of."

"Hmm… nope, sorry. If I think of anything, I'll let you know. I need to go lie down, but you have a nice night, Mark."

He shut the door before Mark even had a chance to reply. Confused by their entire interaction, Mark returned to his car and stood by the driver's side door, trying to make sense of what had just happened. He took a few steps toward the house again, noting that the other windows seemed to be boarded over as well. Between Doug's forced politeness, his wounds, and the windows that had been intentionally sealed shut... something wasn't right.

Unable to shake the feeling that Vanessa's best friend was hiding something, he returned to the front door and knocked again. He considered the possibility that Vanessa had intentionally holed up with Doug, perhaps to hide from the world while she mended her broken heart. He couldn't imagine her quitting her job and leaving everyone to worry about her, though. He knew the idea was unlikely, but he was well beyond desperate. He knocked again and could hear Doug mumbling a string of profanity as he made his way to the door. It cracked open again, and Doug appeared with his fake smile.

"Mark, I know you're worried about Vanessa, but I really need to sleep, okay? If I think of anything, I'll let you know, I promise."

He was in the middle of shutting the door when Mark stopped him by pressing his hand against it and pushing it back open. "Do you mind if I have a look around? It won't take long."

"Not tonight, okay? Maybe tomorrow. Look, I really need to go."

"Harold, let me take a look around his place. It'll only take a second. In and out, I swear."

Doug's demeanor changed in an instant. "Go away, Mark. Don't make me call the cops. They already think you're responsible for her disappearance anyway."

Mark noticed the bloodstain on Doug's side had grown noticeably larger. He used it to call his bluff. "Maybe you should. They can get an ambulance over here for you. You're bleeding pretty good."

Doug seemed to realize he had no other option and reluctantly let Mark in. "Fine, but make it quick."

Mark stepped inside and jerked his chin to the plywood covering the nearest window. "I notice you have them all covered like that. Why?"

"There have been some break-ins in the neighborhood lately. I can't afford bars. I figured that would work." Doug motioned for him to proceed down the hall, and Mark didn't hesitate, having a look around the two small bedrooms before giving the bathroom a glance. No sign of Vanessa. He checked the hallway closet, but it was packed tightly with boxes.

"Is that the attic?" Mark asked, pointing to a pull-down door in the hallway ceiling.

"Oh, for crying out loud," Doug muttered, holding his side. The bloodstain was getting larger. "You really think my best friend is hiding in the attic? Mark, you're being ridiculous. I think it's time for you to go."

"I'm not going anywhere until I see the attic."

Doug sighed and shook his head. "Fine. I'm going to go sit down. I'm feeling lightheaded."

Mark ignored him and pulled the door down; extending the fold-up ladder so he could climb his way up. He turned on the light using its pull chain and stood on the ladder with his head poking into the attic. It was small, with boxes strewn about, and it only took him a few seconds to determine she wasn't there. As he folded the ladder back up and closed the attic door, Doug rushed to his side to usher him out of the house.

"Okay, you've seen enough. Time to leave now," he said, motioning to the front door.

"Show me the basement, and I'm gone."

"No, Mark, enough is enough. I'm not feeding your paranoia anymore. Vanessa's not here. I'm warning you, if you don't leave, I will call the cops."

"Show me the basement," Mark repeated gruffly, his lowered brow reflecting just how serious he was.

"I've shown you everything you need to see. Bedrooms, closets, even my damn attic. You want to check under my kitchen sink, too?"

Mark stared the man down. Doug was sweating profusely and seemed to be holding back his panic. At that moment, he knew Vanessa was in the house.

"The basement. Now," he growled, stepping toward Doug and looking at him menacingly. He towered over the short, portly man and could see him shaking nervously.

"Fine, it's right over there," Doug said, pointing to a door in the corner of the living room.

Mark followed his finger, and the instant he'd looked away, Doug used the chance to strike. He quickly pulled a kitchen knife that he'd been concealing behind his back from the waistband of his pants and stabbed Mark in the chest, lodging the blade there. Mark looked down at the knife handle sticking out from the left breast pocket of his suit jacket with a momentary look of confusion, registering what had happened. It took a second for the pain and shock to set in, and when it did, Mark stumbled back into the wall behind him. Hoping to stab him again, Doug tried to retrieve the knife, but Mark blocked him as he reached for the handle and pushed him back using his right arm. Doug made another attempt at the knife, but Mark pushed back harder and sent the man toppling backward over his coffee table.

Getting stabbed in real life was nothing like it was in the movies or on television. On-screen, a person always seemed to walk off the wound, quickly regaining mobility. Mark was learning firsthand, however, that reality was much different. The cut in his chest was sending blinding pain through his body that worsened when he futilely tried to move his left arm. The blade had severed his pectoral muscle, rendering the entire arm useless. He used his right arm to pull the knife out, roaring in agony as the bloody, four-inch serrated blade did almost as damage coming out as it did going in.

Doug had made his way to his feet, the fall having torn the bandage off of his gut and reopened the wound fully. His shoulder was also bleeding now, confirming that he was also injured there. He tried coming at Mark again but backed away when he realized he no longer had a weapon. Mark took a step forward and swiped the knife at him with his right arm, his left hanging limply by his side.

"Doesn't getting stabbed suck?" Doug wheezed, his shirt heavily soaked in blood.

By now, Mark had put the pieces together. "She stabbed you, didn't she?"

"Vanessa? It was just a lovers' spat. We're fine now. We kissed and made up."

"What did you do with her?" Mark hissed, taking another step toward him.

"How cute. Prince Charming has come to save the day."

They squared off in the living room, both of them bleeding heavily and severely weakened. Even with the gash in his chest, Mark felt he had the advantage. Doug was also having trouble moving his left side, likely from his shoulder injury, and his right side was in rough shape thanks to his wounded gut. He appeared to be having trouble breathing and looked quite close to passing out.

"You're finished," Mark said, holding the knife up defensively. "Give up."

"Everyone always underestimates me," Doug replied with labored breathing. He grabbed a heavy candle from his coffee table, thinking he could use the glass jar it was encased in as a weapon. He lunged at Mark while swinging the large candle, trying to bring it down on his head. Mark sidestepped the attack and swiped the knife at him again, this time catching him across the chest and slicing open his t-shirt. It didn't do much in the way of damage, only making a shallow cut that didn't seem to faze the man.

Doug took another swing with the candle; this time landing a successful blow on Mark's left shoulder. Under normal circumstances, it wouldn't have made much of an impact, but with his wounded chest, it was enough to throw him off balance. Doug seized the chance and brought the candle down again on Mark's head with such force that it shattered the glass jar and dropped Mark to his knees.

"Not so tough now, are you?" Doug taunted, picking up the knife Mark had lost his grip on. Before he could get a chance to use it, Mark grabbed him by the waist and threw him to the floor, rolling on top of him to wrestle the knife from his hand. He succeeded and tossed the bloody blade aside, choosing to finish the man with his fists. He delivered a brutal blow to his face using his good arm and was winding back for another when he heard a muffled female voice from below them.

*"Help me! I'm down here! Help me!"*

It was Vanessa. She'd undoubtedly heard the scuffle taking place upstairs and was screaming frantically. He knocked Doug out with another punch to the face and staggered toward the basement door, his right hand covering the wound in his chest. Feeling faint from the blood he'd lost, he had to rely on his adrenaline and the sound of Vanessa's voice to keep him conscious as he slowly made his way down the stairs, trying not to fall. At the bottom of the stairs, he was greeted by a sturdy locked door and knew he didn't have the strength left in him to search for the keys. Getting down the stairs had been hard enough. Climbing up them to scour the house wasn't going to happen. He summoned the last of his strength and broke the door open with three powerful kicks.

*"Mark!"* he heard Vanessa yell from the darkness. A chain rattled, and she appeared a few feet in front of him, her arms outstretched in an effort to reach for him. There was enough light shining in from the open basement door for him to see that she'd been stopped by a padlocked chain wrapped around her waist. He

fumbled for the light switch next to him and turned it on, tears forming in his eyes at the sight of his love, still alive and in one piece. The blood loss combined with the emotion of seeing Vanessa proved too much, and he collapsed on the floor in front of her, just out of her grasp.

"Mark, Mark, stay with me!" Vanessa cried, kneeling and reaching for him. "Stay with me, baby."

Her words brought him back to life. He couldn't give up now, not when they were so close. He fought off the blackness threatening to engulf him and noticed a bent metal folding chair leaning against the wall behind him. He kicked it over with his foot and reached for it, using it to help him get to his feet. Still woozy, he used the chair as a walker while Vanessa guided him to the cot.

"Lay down," she instructed, helping him onto it gently. She took a seat next to him and held his hand, clenching it tightly as he looked up at her.

"Vanessa," he said weakly. "I found you."

"Shh… don't speak, baby. Save your energy. We need to get you to a hospital."

"My phone… it's in my pocket," he breathed.

She dug into his pants and pulled out his cell phone, quickly dialing 911 and insisting they hurry. With assurance they were on their way, she set the phone aside and took Mark's hand again. "Just hold on, okay? They'll be here soon."

"I'm... I'm sorry I lied to you."

"It's okay, sweetie. Don't you even worry about that now? Just stay with me. Help is on the way."

"Doug was right," he said, cracking a slight smile. "Getting stabbed sucks."

She chuckled, taking his humor as a good sign. "He'd definitely know. I got him good today. Twice."

"I saw that," he nodded. "I'm proud of you."

They turned their heads at the sound of somebody clumsily making their way down the stairs, banging into the walls as they tried to stay on their feet. Doug appeared in the doorway holding the kitchen knife and looking like he'd been hit by a truck. His face was bloody and already bruised from the punches Mark had laid him out with, his shirt more red than gray. Blood dripped to the floor as he looked at them with his left eye, his right eye swollen shut.

"Surprise," he smirked, swaying back and forth like a drunk person.

"Jesus…" Vanessa muttered at the sight of him. "How are you even still alive?"

"I'm resilient. What can I say?" he chuckled, then turned his head to spit blood onto the floor.

Mark tried to speak, but his voice was faint and shaky. "The… cops… are on their…"

"I'm sorry, what was that?" Doug smiled, taking joy in how much damage he'd caused him.

"He said the cops are on their way, asshole," Vanessa reiterated. "Just give up. You're done."

"We could have been so happy together, you know that?" Doug said, ignoring her comment as he slowly crossed the room to them. "We still can be. Just not here. Not in this life."

She stood up, ready to defend herself. Mark nudged her side and pointed to the metal folding chair they'd left next to the cot. She grabbed it and readied it to swing. "Stay back, Doug, I'm warning you."

He raised the knife and took another step toward her. "I never wanted to hurt you. You know that, right?"

*"Stay back!"*

"But you haven't given me any choice. I'll make it quick, I promise. I love you, Vanessa. I don't want you to suffer. Him, on the other hand," he said, nodding at Mark, "I'm going to make sure his death is painful."

He moved closer and tried to jab her with the knife, but he was too slow. She stepped aside and swung the chair, hitting him over the head so hard it bent the chair even farther out of shape. He fell to the floor and tried to get up, but she wasn't going to afford him the chance. Releasing all of her anger, she cocked back and hit him again, screaming as she continued to hit him until he lay lifeless by her feet, his skull completely caved in.

Her shoulders hitched, and her chest heaved as she sobbed. Still holding the chair, now covered with blood, she looked down at the body of her former best friend. She was overwhelmed with emotions, many of them conflicting, but didn't have time to sort them out now. Mark needed her. She threw the chair aside and returned to his side, brushing a strand of hair from his face.

"Remind me to never piss you off," he smirked.

She chuckled, but it was more out of relief that he was still alive. "I don't think he's getting up from that one."

"I love you, Vanessa," he told her, still fighting to stay awake.

"I love you, too."

Seconds later, the police swarmed the place with paramedics following behind. Knowing Vanessa was safe, Mark allowed himself to slip into darkness.

# Epilogue
## *Mark and Vanessa*

"Morning, baby," Vanessa yawned, rolling over and cuddling up next to him. He wrapped his arm around her, and she traced the scar on his chest, something she found herself doing often. The scar was a permanent reminder of what had happened. It had become beautiful to her, serving as a reflection of Mark's unwavering love for her and his resolve to find her, no matter the cost.

"There's my pretty wife," he purred, kissing her forehead. He placed his hand on her belly and smiled. "And there's my little man."

"Or your little girl," Vanessa laughed, playfully swatting his shoulder.

"I'll be the happiest man alive either way."

Mark had been lucky. The doctors had told him that if his chest muscles hadn't been so large and so dense, the knife would have pierced his heart and surely killed him. After a few days in the hospital, he was released and spent his time recovering in his townhouse with Vanessa looking after him.

Vanessa, traumatized from the ordeal, had agreed to counseling and had been seeing a therapist. She still had nightmares and would wake screaming, convinced she was locked in Doug's basement, but Mark was always there to console her. He'd take her in his arms and rub her back; letting her cry it out as he assured her she was safe. He'd suggested they take a break from New York to spend the winter at his second home in Los Angeles. She'd agreed it was a good idea since the media had picked up the story and had been relentless in their coverage, shoving microphones in their faces and pestering them for interviews every chance they got.

It had come to light that Doug had gotten into trouble in high school after fixating on a classmate and subsequently stalking her. As with Vanessa, he'd begun harassing the girl through unrelenting text messages. It had culminated with her calling the cops, but since Doug was a minor at the time, he'd only received a slap on the wrist, and the records had been sealed. If Michael McKeever had been able to access the information, Mark was sure he would have been able to rescue her sooner. He didn't hold it against the man since no private investigator would have been able to get those records.

In the three months since the incident, Mark had never left her side. He took a long leave from work to be there for her, hiring somebody to oversee his regular duties. Whisking her away to Paris for Valentine's Day, they spent a week exploring the romantic city, and he'd surprised her by proposing by the Eiffel Tower. She eagerly agreed, thrilled at the prospect of marrying the man who'd refused to give up on her. The man who'd risked his life to save her and bore the scar that she'd kiss every night before bed.

They married one month later on a beach in Hawaii. It was a small ceremony with Linda and Vanessa's mother among the few in attendance. Mark, who'd been overjoyed with the news of Vanessa's pregnancy, vowed to always be there for her and the child. In return, Vanessa made light of their history by vowing never to get kidnapped again. They spent their honeymoon in a posh resort off the coast of Honolulu, enjoying the sun and warm weather during the day and making love on the beach at night.

Now, back in Mark's modern Los Angeles home, Vanessa rolled on top of her hero husband and covered him with kisses. "I love you, Fitness Mark."

He laughed at the inside joke they only shared behind closed doors and tickled her sides. "Very funny, Nessa Baby."

She squealed in laughter, then turned the tables on him by grinding her hips into him as she straddled his lap. Feeling his cock growing harder under her, she smirked, "This is getting your attention, isn't it?"

"Maybe just a little," he smiled.

"It feels like a lot." She pulled off her shirt and tossed it aside.

"Goddamn, you're sexy," he breathed, admiring her body.

"You still going to find me sexy in a few months when I'm super pregnant?"

"Of course." He grinned and added, "You need to pump that baby out already so I can put another one in you."

"Really?" she asked, pulling his cock out of his boxer briefs and stroking it gently. "You're planning to get me knocked up again already?"

He moaned at her touch. "The thought crossed my mind, yes."

She pulled her panties aside and slid him inside of her. "I guess we better start practicing, then."